To Daffeny:

A solid sister and a great educator.

Hugh H. Weathers

C.A.N.

PULP COLORED
THE MILKMAN

BY

HUGH M. WEATHERS

Ph.D

Copyright © 2014 Hugh M. Weathers, Ph.D.

All rights reserved. No part of this book may be reproduced, stored, or transmitted by any means—whether auditory, graphic, mechanical, or electronic—without written permission of both publisher and author, except in the case of brief excerpts used in critical articles and reviews. Unauthorized reproduction of any part of this work is illegal and is punishable by law.

ISBN: 978-1-4834-1959-6 (sc)
ISBN: 978-1-4834-1958-9 (e)

Library of Congress Catalog Number: TXU 1174382

Cover Art and Graphics: Cori Gray

Additional Artwork: Ron Chase

Because of the dynamic nature of the Internet, any web addresses or links contained in this book may have changed since publication and may no longer be valid. The views expressed in this work are solely those of the author and do not necessarily reflect the views of the publisher, and the publisher hereby disclaims any responsibility for them.

Any people depicted in stock imagery provided by Thinkstock are models, and such images are being used for illustrative purposes only.
Certain stock imagery © Thinkstock.

Lulu Publishing Services rev. date: 12/11/2014

This is dedicated to my parents:

**MARY FRANCES WEATHERS AND
DAVID WEATHERS, SR.**

Immeasurable appreciation is bestowed upon the following:

C. Perry for the tireless hours spent on this project

Doris Reed for her love and support

AND

A Special thanks to

Mr. Bill Duke

for his encouragement, support, positive dialog and artistic direction

Contents

Chapter 1	The Beginning	1
Chapter 2	Thirty Years Later	3
Chapter 3	Meeting with the Mayor	19
Chapter 4	Restaurant	24
Chapter 5	City Hall	30
Chapter 6	Abuse	39
Chapter 7	Hospital	46
Chapter 8	Headquarters	53
Chapter 9	Stakeout	56
Chapter 10	The Chase	59
Chapter 11	House Crashers	69
Chapter 12	The Connection	87
Chapter 13	The Plan	98
Chapter 14	Implementation	102
Chapter 15	Home Coming	114
Chapter 16	The Grave	118

Chapter One

THE BEGINNING

Picture this: A hot Saturday morning in Washington D.C. a little black boy sitting on a couch in his living room area watching an old style black & white T. V. with rabbit ears. His legs are crossed with his feet on an old scratched up coffee table. He is wearing a pair of red & black cowboy boots, a cowboy hat and is pretending to smoke an old style pipe.

His mother, Margret, a black woman, is in the kitchen dressed in an old style white nurse's uniform with matching hat. She yells out loud, "Boy, you have been watching TV all morning long. You are going to turn into a TV and quit trying to smoke your father's pipe." Margret walks over to a wall in the kitchen, stares at a picture of a very good looking black man wearing a white milkman's uniform, tie and hat and is standing in front of a milk truck. Margret, continuing to stare at the man in the picture says to her son, "Don't forget to drink all of your milk."

Chapter Two

THIRTY YEARS LATER

In a bigger and better apartment, the living situation has improved with central air, ceiling fans, wall to wall carpeting, modern furniture and appliances. The boy has now turned into a grown man., C.A.N. He is sitting in the same position, legs crossed, watching T.V wearing a tailored made suit, shirt & tie, matching suspenders, crocodile shoes, and smoking what looks like a crack pipe.

On a wide screen high definition T.V. C.A.N. is watching a scene from the movie, **Outlaw Josey Wales**, where Clint Eastwood says, 'You boys going to pull them pistols or whistle Dixie?' The movie ends. C.A.N. turns the T.V. channel to the local news. A young, white female newscaster elaborates about armed gangsters having robbed a community bank that services the local head start program, seniors citizens, merchants and the 501c3's, etc. Getting up off the couch, C.A.N. goes into the closet and opens up an old white suitcase that has a picture of a milk bottle on the cover. He pulls out several guns. Putting them under his suit jacket, he leaves the apartment. He walks the streets asking questions of people that he knows as to where to find the gang who robbed the community bank. Through physical persuasion he is able to find out who they are and where to find them.

C.A.N. finds the gang members hiding out in a very expensive and lavish apartment building in northwest. The gangsters are a mixed culture of young men who are organized, money-hungry, ruthless, dope dealers. They are well dressed and surrounded by young pretty girls. Their apartment is extravagantly furnished with all the upscale amenities including music and entertainment. Some of the members are sitting at the dining room table counting the money they stole from the community bank. Others are watching T.V. and playing video games while still others are in the back room having wild sex with the pretty girls.

Reaching into his pocket, C.A.N. pulls out pick lock tools and quietly picks the lock on the door and eases his way into the apartment unnoticed at first while gang members are sitting at the table counting money. He stands in the middle of the floor smoking his glass pipe connected to a gold chain around his neck. He watches three of the gang members and a girl sitting at the table counting their loot. The girl looks up and notices him standing there. She uses her elbow to bump and nudge the member sitting next to her at the head of the table holding money in his hand, smoking a cigar and is startled and surprised to see C.A.N. The one member at the head of the table, still sitting, stunned and bewildered says to C.A.N., "Can I help you mister?" He pauses for a second then says, "And how in the hell did you get in here?"

Not answering, C.A.N. loads up his pipe with what appears to be a white rock, lights it with his old fashioned gold cigarette lighter, takes a puff and blows out a heavy white cloud of smoke. Sweat appears on his forehead and on his eyebrow, but he still does not answer.

One of the gang members sitting at the table says, "That nigger's crazy!"

The gang member sitting at the head of the table asks, "You got a problem, nigger?"

The other members get up very slowly from the table while opening their suit jackets so C.A.N. can see they have guns. The guns are under their armpits being held by shoulder straps. The girl and the head gang member stay seated. C.A.N. looks at all the members directly in their eyes and says, "You boys going to pull them pistols or whistle Dixie?" The members reach for their guns while the seated one reaches for his gun as he stands. The girl ducks under the table. As other members reach for their guns C.A.N. quickly releases the pipe from his hands which is held with a gold chain around his neck keeping it from falling to the floor. Moving quickly before the gang members can shoot, C.A.N. pulls two nice fancy gold plated pistols from his waist and begins blasting away – shooting each gang member before they could shoot him. The bullets are hitting the table and the loot flies through the air. Bullets are flying around the room hitting stereos, blowing up T.Vs. and striking light fixtures. Two of the members are blown back against the wall. The head member falls on the table and his cigar flips out of his mouth into the air. C.A.N. catches the cigar with his mouth and takes a puff.

The members having sex in the back bedroom stop their activity when they hear the shooting. One of the girls dives under the bed and the other runs into the closet. With weapons drawn, the men with their backs against the wall walk slowly down the hall toward the front of the apartment. They get to the front of the apartment to find it shot up and see their friends sprawled across the room.

C.A.N, however, is not anywhere in sight. They hear a noise under the table and with their guns still drawn they look under the table and find the girl scared, nervous and shaking. They pull her from beneath the table and ask, "What the hell happened? Who did this?"

"Some crazy ass nigger appeared out of nowhere and just started shooting."

Another member asks, "What nigger? Where is he now? Where did he go?"

Nervously she responds, "How in the hell should I know? I am getting the hell out of here!"

She turns and runs out of the apartment slamming the door. After the door slams, the members hear a crunching noise coming from the kitchen. They creep towards the kitchen and see C.A.N. sitting at the table eating a bowl of honey and oats cereal. The loud crunching is from him eating the cereal without milk.

Gang member, Steve says, "You must be the crazy ass nigger that was doing all that shooting."

Alvero says, "Yo, nigger, you shot up our people!"

C.A.N., sitting at the table in a calm, cool and collective manner says, "You got milk?"

Steve screams, "What? Milk? Nigger, what the hell you think this is Dairy Queen?" All of the members laugh hysterically.

Alvero chimes in, "Milk is for kids, fool."

C.A.N. calmly responds, "You niggers haven't got any milk. Without milk these oats are driving this kid mad."

Alvero looking at Steve asks, "Who is this crazy ass nigger talking shit about some damn milk? Let's just blast his crazy ass."

Thirty Years Later

On the words *crazy ass*, C.A.N. quickly dumps the table over, the bowl and cereal fly in the air while pulling his pistols he shoots at will. The gang members are shooting back but their bullets are missing C.A.N. hitting the refrigerator, microwave, toaster and stove. The cabinet doors fly open and bullets hit dishes and glasses. C.A.N. is blasting back while using the table as a cover shield. The members run out of bullets and drop their pistols attempting to reload. Hearing the member's weapons drop C.A.N. quickly reloads his pistols using automatic reloaders and blasts the members before they can start shooting again. Members fall to the floor landing on top of each other forming a human mountain. C.A.N. consciously moves toward the gang members lying on top of each other on the kitchen floor. While standing over their bodies admiring his work, he hears movement in the back bedroom where the two girls are hiding. With guns drawn and his back against the wall he walks slowly down the hall towards the noise. Not knowing where the girls are located, he enters the bedroom and hears a girl breathing hard under the bed unaware there is another hiding in the closet. He looks under the bed and sees a pretty young girl. She is very nervous and scared.

The girl hiding in the closet is very quiet with her hand on the trigger of a gun pointed right at him as she watches his every move. She is about to squeeze the trigger but stops when she sees C.A.N.'s bright cheerful smile and soft handling of her friend as he helps her from beneath the bed. In a calm, peaceful and warm voice C.A.N. says to the girl who was under the bed, "Everything is going to be alright, darling. Nothing is going to harm you now, Precious." He rubs her pretty face, and pulls back her long hair and flips it over her shoulders kissing her ever so softly and gently.

Seeing that C.A.N. is trying to be nice, she begins to calm down relaxing and catching her breath. C.A.N. continues to kiss her hand, her arm and moves up to her shoulder. Still a little nervous, she begins to get into his moves. C.A.N kisses her neck, shoulders, chest and breast. He kisses her flat stomach and shapely legs along with her pretty feet. The girl in the closet begins to relax a little after she sees her friend begins to somewhat relax, calm down and enjoy what

C.A.N. is doing with passion and not using brute force. C.A.N. and the girl begin to make passionate love. Still watching carefully, the girl in the closet begins to remove her finger from the trigger of the gun. Watching C.A.N. and her girlfriend making love, the girl in the closet begins to get turned on and uses her fingers and gun to rub her breast and stomach in a smooth and circular motion. She masturbates with the pistol moving the pistol in and out of her vagina and backside while rubbing and massaging her clitoris with her free hand. This action goes on for a few minutes. Then the girl emerges from the closet. She startles C.A.N. for a few seconds at first because he sees the gun in her hand, but she smiles and puts the gun down which helped ease his tension. He sees that the girl from the closet has very large breast and says, "Milk!" He begins to suck on her breasts and pulls her into the bed. They all join in to have sex. C.A.N. still with his nice clothes on but pants and underwear down by his ankles is making love to the girl on the bottom while the other girl from the closet is riding his back with her arms around his neck and shoulders. He switches back and forth, spinning around making love to the girl on the bottom and spinning around quickly to make love to the girl riding his back.

While he switches to making love to the girl riding his back, the girl on the bottom is licking his ear, biting his neck and squeezes his chest and his private parts. They are getting it on with hot, steamy sex.

The girl who ran out of the apartment before the second round of shooting began called the police from her cellphone to report the incident. She tells the 911 operator that she was concerned about her two girlfriends that she left in the apartment. The police officers and CSI personnel arrive on the scene to evaluate the madness. The police and investigators discuss and exchange points of view, opinions and analysis on how such a crazy thing could have happen. They cannot come to terms or understand the significance or reason for the cereal and bowl on the floor without any signs of milk and the dead bodies everywhere.

Lead investigator, Mr. Sheen says, "The person eating the cereal must have been in a hurry … they ate the cereal without milk." Staring at the bowl, Sheen says, "Man, that would choke me to death. Hey, those two victims look like the two men that were identified by the police composite sketch who were major suspects in that robbery that occurred earlier today."

O'Malley, the second investigator asks, "You think there is a link?"

"It's too early to make that determination at this stage. We must first find the shooter and try to link him or her to this crime," Sheen responds. "We need to question the young lady who placed the call."

He locates the girl who placed the call. Sabrina tells Sheen, "When the shooting started I crawled to the door and ran for my life." Sheen later located the other two young ladies and questioned them.

"You young ladies better start talking now or else you'll be going to jail for a long time. People died in that apartment."

The girl that dove under the bed when the shooting started began, "We don't know what happened. We were in the back when we heard the shooting and I hid under the bed."

The closet girl says, "I hid in the closet."

"Did you all see or hear anything at all? Did the shooter say anything? Did you even hear his voice?"

One girl spoke up, "I think the man said something about whistling Dixie."

"Whistling Dixie?"

"Yeah. He said something like you boys going to pull them pistols or whistle Dixie and that's when the shooting started."

As the police and investigators leave the scene, O'Malley asked Sheen, "Whistling Dixie, what the hell is that all about?"

"Outlaw Josey Wales."

O'Malley, still puzzled, "Outlaw Josey Wales, what is that?"

"A movie before your time, kid."

By this time C.A.N. is back at home in his apartment sitting in front of his T.V. watching another crime scene on the network news with that pipe hanging from the chain around his neck. The news announcer is explaining that 'the suspected drug dealers were shot and killed last night in a hail of gunfire. Among those killed were women and children believed to be innocent victims. Due to the nature of the crime, authorities suspect organized crime or rival gang members are responsible. Outraged community leaders and political activists have banned together to show moral support for the families of the innocent victims. They demand better police protection for the community. They further demand swift action be taken to bring a halt to the drug activity and robberies in the community.'

Interviewed by the newscaster, Rev. Henderson stated that, "The resident council will schedule a meeting between community leaders and the authorities to implement strategies to ensure that positive action is taken to expedite change in the community."

C.A.N. continues to watch the news broadcast when a commercial comes on advertising Dunkin Donuts. The commercial includes the Dunkin Donuts man saying, "It's time to make the donuts."

C.A.N. leaves his apartment wearing a nice pinstripe suit to find the mobsters that killed the innocent family members mentioned on the news. While walking down the street he encounters a fast food deliveryman wearing the same color outfit similar to that of the Dunkin Donut man in the commercial.

The two men bump into each other and the innocent physical contact causes the deliveryman to drop the four pizza boxes to the pavement. The deliveryman in a Hispanic dialect says, "Hey mister, are you fucking blind? You ruined my delivery. This is the biggest delivery I've had all week. I suppose you are not going to pay for it now."

C.A.N., while helping the deliveryman up from the ground says, "Where were you going with all that food?"

"Upstairs in this building."

"I'll tell you what I'm going to do. I will pay you for the food and your clothes, including that hat."

"I need my clothes man. I just need to cover the food so that my boss won't fire me."

"How much for the food?"

"Fifty dollars."

"How much for the suit and hat?"

"Hey man, like I told you I need my clothes."

C.A.N. drags the deliveryman into the alley and takes his clothes, leaving him two one hundred dollar bills. He picks up the food stuffing it back into the delivery boxes. He looks very funny in the delivery clothes and the hat that is two sizes too small as he walks down the street with the boxes. He keeps on his expensive crocodile shoes and silk socks. He looks like a nerd wearing sharp shoes.

C.A.N. goes into the building with the food delivery, walks up the stairs to the third floor where mob members are inside and rings the doorbell. A member dressed in a very expensive suit, shirt & tie comes to the door with gun in hand and says as he looks through the peephole, "Who is it?"

C.A.N., while head leaning forward towards the peephole says, "Pizza."

The mob member looks through the peephole, sees C.A.N.'s hat and opens the door slowly. As soon as the door is opened wide enough, C.A.N. rushes inside, stumbles forward and knocks the member down but still holding onto the boxes.

Standing upright, C.A.N waits for the member to get to his feet. Meanwhile, other members observe the commotion while two of them stand putting their hands on their guns. The member getting up from the floor says, "You crazy ass nigger! What the hell you think you are doing?"

Everyone is looking on in amazement. Some are half smiling and laughing at the episode because of the way C.A.N. is dressed (looking like a nerd). C.A.N. continues to stand.

The mob member who got up from the floor takes the food from the man's hand and says, "I hope you don't think you're getting a tip."

Another chimes in saying, "You're lucky we didn't fucking kill you."

The mob member who was on the floor says: "What are you standing there for?

Are you fucking crazy or what? You ain't getting a tip."

C.A.N. says, as he looks at his watch, "Do you know what time it is?"

"Time? Nigger, it's time for you to leave while you still can." Everybody laughs. C.A.N remains still. The member, looking puzzled says, "Ok, nigger, you've stumped us. What time is it?"

C.A.N. screams out loud, "It's time to make the motherfucking donuts." Catching mob members off guard, he quickly pulls out two high tech automatic weapons that shoot powerful bullets blasting members as they scatter, duck and run. He screams out loud while he blasts his weapons, "Y'all want to murder innocent colored folk over some devils powder. You are sorry sons-of-bitches."

The shootout continues. Those who escaped being shot try shooting back as they run for cover, diving under tables, behind couches and into the backrooms. C.A.N. is blasting furiously. The powerful bullets are going through the tables and walls killing the mob members as they flee while trying to shoot back.

There are two remaining mob members hiding in the back trying to figure out what the fuck is going on.

"Who and where is that crazy ass nigger?"

"I don't know. I can't see him. Take a look. Find out where he is."

"Fuck that! You look. I'm going to find a way out of here."

Murmuring to himself in a soft tone he says, "Fine. I will find that crazy ass nigger and I'll kill him myself." He walks slowly out of the backroom looking for C.A.N. but sees no sight of him.

Suddenly he hears noises in the room he just left. He hears his friend begging for his life. Running back to help he finds his friend hanging from the ceiling.

He looks around to find C.A.N. standing nearby with guns aimed at him. C.A.N. puts one of his guns at the mob member's throat and walks him into the kitchen and makes him open the refrigerator door.

Looking inside the refrigerator searching he finds a bottle of milk. Removing the milk from the refrigerator he takes a drink. C.A.N. standing looking at the member with the gun still at his throat while drinking the milk says, "Y'all did a lot of harm to some decent folk. I am going to let you live so you can make it right. If you don't make it right, I <u>will</u> visit you again."

Scared, nervous and sweaty he asks, "Make what right? What the hell you talking about? What do you want me to do?" C.A.N does not answer and backs out of the apartment slowly drinking milk with one hand and pointing the gun at the lone mob member with the other.

After C.A.N leaves, the lone survivor looks around the apartment at all the damage with his pals lying there shot up wondering what just happened and how it happened.

The same investigators as before arrive on the scene with police officers roping off the area.

The lead investigator, Sheen, questions the only surviving member as police and representatives from the coroner's office put the bodies in bags. As usual, investigators are looking over the scene taking pictures.

Sheen, looking at the stunned individual, states, "Mr. you have some explaining to do. We need to know what happen here? This place looks like a hurricane struck it."

The member shrieks, "Some crazy ass nig." Before he can finish his sentence, Sheen gives him a funny look. The mobster continues, "I mean some black man came in here and just started shooting for no reason."

O'Malley asks, "What's up with the man hanging in the back?"

"We were hiding in the back and I thought that the crazy nig, I mean crazy fool was gone, so I went to leave, and heard a noise in the back where I had just left. When I went back to see what it was I found Jimmy hanging there. The man put a gun to my throat and walk me to the refrigerator, took some milk and left."

"Let me understand you correctly, this man who just showed up out of nowhere, shot up the place, killed these men and drank some milk and left? Right? How did he get in?" Sheen asked.

"We all thought he was the delivery boy with our food."

Sheen asked, "delivery boy?"

"Yeah, he screamed something about making donuts."

O'Malley questioned, "Donuts?"

The mobster stated angrily, "Don't worry about it. I'll handle it. I'll find that crazy ass nigger."

Sheen looking at the mob member says, "Let the police handle it. Let the police do their jobs."

Clearing the scene, the police get the bodies put into wagons and hauled away while investigators retreat to their cars. O'Malley says, "Time to make the donuts. Which movie is that from?"

"Not a movie," Sheen said. "That was a commercial. But I still can't make a connection with the milk."

C.A.N. is back at home sitting on the couch watching T.V. The movie is **"Gladiator"** and the scene is Russell Crow saying, "Are you not entertained?"

After the movie ends, the local news covers a story about how a Negro College Fund community event fundraiser was robbed by several men in masks. The robbers shot up the banquet hall killing security guards and took black dignitaries as hostages using them as shields as a part of their get-away plan. The report states that the robbers got away in a van placing hostages in front of the windows of the van to use as shields.

It was also reported the police pursued the robbers and their hostages on a wild chase through the city. During the chase, Kelly, the head of the gang, yells out the van window telling the pursuing police officers that he will kill all of the hostages if they don't back off and halt their pursuit.

Over the police scanner Sheen tells the pursuing police to back off and to stop the pursuit.

Kelly directs his crew to take the hostages to their hideout.

In a supped-up Lincoln Town car C.A.N. has been following the van from a safe distance out of the view of the robbers and police.

Back at the hideout, the hostage's faces are pale with fear and bodies trembling from fright. One of the hostages, an elderly black man nervously says to one of the robbers, "You all don't need us anymore. Can we go now? We can find our way back."

Kelly explains to the hostages that he will let them all go when tension eases up and things cool off and there are no cops in sight. Kelly also tells the hostages, "You all just remain calm. Stay together where we can see you and if the police keep their promise we will let you all go."

The robbers step away from the hostages to huddle to discuss their plans and strategize their next move.

Meanwhile, C.A.N. shows up at the hideout, well dressed with the pipe around his neck. He uses pick locks to ease his way into the room where the hostages are being held. The elderly black man is the only person to see C.A.N. ease his way into the room. After slipping into the room, C.A.N. is able to mingle with the hostages who are still frighten.

Unaware that C.A.N. has slipped into the room, Kelly says, "I thought I told all you people to stay together." Kelly then stares at C.A.N., realizes that he looks unfamiliar and a little different from the rest of the hostages and says, "I don't recognize you. Why aren't you over there with the rest of them?"

C.A.N. strongly and firmly says, "Let my people go."

Kelly replies, "I have to give it to you mister, you sure have some balls. Now get your black ass over there with the rest of them."

C.A.N. repeats, "Let my people go."

Kelly, laughing, says, "Are you fucking retarded, crazy, or do you have a death wish or something? I will tell you what I'm going to do." And with two of the other robbers standing there smiling, Kelly says, "If you can get through my men, like Moses parted the sea I will let your people go." All of the robbers laugh.

C.A.N. says to Kelly while looking at the elderly black man, "When I finish scalding these hogs and grinding up this pork you will let my people go." C.A.N. pauses for a second and says, "And you better have some milk." He looks over at the hostages and says, "It's time to part the sea."

Kelly and his robbers are puzzled and slightly angered as they approach C.A.N. A vicious and ferocious battle of hand-to-hand combat without guns break out between the robbers and C.A.N. The hostages stay clear and look on in fear and amazement. The battle continues for about five minutes with the robbers getting the best of C.A.N. and from time to time rebounding and him getting the best of them. C.A.N is evenly matched in strength with each of the robbers, but appears to be the quickest and swiftest of them all. The hostages continue to look on in shock and awe as the battle swings back and forth, until the robbers began to tire and slow down. The battle begins to turn in favor of C.A.N. He begins to win the fistfight, getting the best of the robbers as they tire. One of the robbers takes a last stand with a wild punch that misses C.A.N. but accidentally hits the elderly black man and knocks him into some of the hostages as they fall to the floor.

After conquering all but two of the robbers, C.A.N. puts the remaining two in a headlock. He has a robber under each of his arm pits squeezing their necks to a point where they are almost chocking to death. C.A.N. looks up at Kelly as he holds the two robbers in the chokeholds and screams, "Are you not entertained?" The hostages and Kelly are now speechless. Then he yells to Kelly, "Let my people go!"

With a frightening look on his face, Kelly shouts, "You all get the hell out of here and take that crazy ass nigger with you." The hostages immediately make their way out of the building while some move slowly as they help the elderly black man.

C.A.N. looks at Kelly says, "Milk?"

Kelly, "It's in the cooler. Take all you want."

Sheen arrives on the scene and questions Kelly as the investigators lead him away. Kelly explains to Sheen, "He followed us here somehow. He must have been on something to man handle my boys like that."

Sheen asked Kelly, "Did he say anything?"

"Yeah. He kept telling us to let his people go and when he went through my boys he asked me if I was entertained."

"Did he demand milk?"

"Yes. That crazy ass … he took milk from the cooler. Sounds like you know this man."

As the investigators were leaving the scene, O'Malley says, "I know that movie. That one is **Gladiator**."

"You are right," Sheen chirps.

"This man is into all kind of movies. When does he have time to watch TV?" O'Malley asks with a sincere level of curiosity.

"He is very clever and slick to sneak up on those bad guys like that."

"He must be in very good shape to take on guys like that and win, especially being out numbered."

"Or he is on something. I still can't make the connection with the milk."

"Man, maybe I need to start drinking that stuff."

"Why?"

"I don't know. It seems to be working for him."

"It might be what's making him crazy. Do you want that? I am going crazy trying to figure this man out".

Back at home C.A.N. is in his favorite position watching T.V. Another news station is reporting on a story about a crazed mad man wreaking havoc on bad guys who had done harm to innocent citizens. During each attack, he allowed one bad guy to live for some particular reason.

C.A.N. turns to another channel where there is a news story about the 'crazed man' having struck again and in each episode he always leaves one survivor. The police say that they are not sure why he leaves a survivor.

C.A.N. flips to another channel to hear the news reporter state, "The mad man is still out there finding the bad guys that the police are unable to locate and punishing the bad guys with terror. It is not clear at this time if this man is leaving one survivor on purpose or if it is just luck for the lone survivor. All of the witnesses who survive the attacks are repeating the same story about the crazed man demanding milk. Now let's go to the street with our reporter, Janet Lee. Janet what do you have for us?"

"Well, believe it or not Jim, this so-called mad man or lunatic has earned a group of followers. Something like a cult who follows his every move. The followers say they support what he is doing. They even have T-Shirts with pictures of milk bottles on them."

"Why is that Janet?"

"Jim, they say it is because he is doing to the bad guys what the bad guys have done to innocent people. They also believe this man is doing what needs to be done so citizens can feel safe … sort of like a judge and jury. Jim, another result of the mad man's terror is many of the citizens of this city are carrying around extra bottles of milk in the event they run into him. They feel milk seems to be the key to their safety." The news pans the streets showing citizens walking with bottles of milk in tote bags and on the sides of briefcases.

C.A.N. switches channels and sees a news personality interviewing an East Indian man who owns a convenience store. In a heavy East Indian accent the man says, "In my store, milk was not a big seller, but now I can't keep it on the shelves. I am not complaining because it is good for my business. I await the arrival of the truck so that I can restock the shelves."

A shot of an eighteen-wheeler carrying milk appears on screen and is being shown being forced over and high-jacked by a bunch of non-criminal looking culturally mixed community people. They pulled the driver out who is a young, white female.

They yell, "We aren't criminals and we aren't going to hurt you. We just want the milk."

Being interviewed by the news reporter the driver explains, "They were nice people. They just wanted the milk because they said the stores always run out. They wanted to get to it first."

Chapter Three

MEETING WITH THE MAYOR

Mayor Steve Smith, a young black, well-educated man in his early fifties, and popular amongst the majority is having a conversation with the Chief of Police, Sally Stewart. Stewart is in her early forties and comes from a long lineage of police officers. They are having a conversation about this local hero that the citizens are now calling the "Milk Man".

Stewart ask Smith, "Who is this mad man performing destruction and mayhem on the bad guys while seeking revenge for the people we are supposed to protect and serve? Do we have a clue to who this lunatic may be, and why it is that we always seem to be one step behind him? Your honor?"

"You can call me Steve."

"Steve, our investigators have informed me that this man is watching movies and commercials on T.V. During the altercations with the criminals he recites verses from these movies and commercials. He is vicariously living a hero's fantasy which makes him feel that he is saving the world by challenging the bad guys who do harm to innocent people. According to the experts, when the citizens are on the bandwagon it gives him worthiness through psychological re-enforcement. This action also makes him somewhat predictable."

"Movies and commercials, Chief? What in the name of Kafka are you talking about? Now you have told me what he does, can you tell me who he is and how you intend to catch this fool before we both lose our jobs? And if he is predictable, you should be able to catch him."

The Chief asserted, "I assure you Mayor, we are working on it."

"Regarding this fool, there are a group of higher-ups, I mean political troublemakers that think that you are incompetent. So do us both a favor and find this fool as of yesterday and make us both look good."

"As we speak, I have my best investigators on this case. I have all the confidence that they will be able to bring this maniac down."

The Mayor sighs, "Good. That's music to my ears. Chief, even though he is winning the support of some of the residents in this city, (hell, even my granddaughter has one of them damn T-shirts) I don't want people to think this type of behavior should be rewarded or tolerated. I don't want to encourage people to take matters into their own hands or let other maniacs attempt to copycat this madness."

"Mayor, there is one more issue at hand."

"Oh, what is that?"

"The media, the press and the coverage and attention given to this situation seems to generate more support for this maniac. This doesn't work in our favor."

"Being a member of the press many years ago and having your job just a few years ago, I do believe that my office and I can handle the press. You tell the press that your department is working on a plan, but do not, I repeat, do not give them the name of your lead investigator, reveal or spell out your plan. We do not want to put your people in further danger. If the media continues to hound you, order your people to direct the media to my office."

"From what I heard, you were a damn good cop and a smart one too. I plan to follow in your footsteps."

"That's why I appointed you, Sally."

"Do we have a plan?" Sally inquires.

"Yes. Put together a taskforce to work in conjunction with the media. Include the cable networks too. Get a list of their subscribers and movie schedules then cross reference that list with offenders and other psychos that fit the profile of this fool. See if the networks can pinpoint what households or districts are watching which movies. Try to get dates and time slots. There has to be a way to narrow it down to an area where this fool is living or at least eliminate areas where he is not."

"Kind of like the Nielson rating ... assuming he's living in a house or an apartment with an address, right?"

"If he is watching reruns, we can focus on the network that shows a lot of re-runs."

"You know there is an undercurrent of thought by certain members of the City Council. They do not want this mad man caught. Statistically speaking, since this whole thing started, crime-related activity in the city has been reduced dramatically by 60%. Certain members of the Council, the so-called spin doctors want to put a political spin on it and take credit for the reduction."

"What they want is your job and my head on a political platter, Sally. As a team, you and I will put our own spin on it and make the numbers work for us. Chief, you really need to bring this fool in and prosecute him. Prosecute him on T.V. if we can. Upon his capture we need to implement a new strategy that will keep the crime activity down. I will write an appropriation for more funding to ensure its implementation."

Chief Stewart organizes a taskforce to include O'Malley and Sheen as well as a team of investigators to visit the network stations and cable companies to obtain demographics, program itineraries and scheduling. One of the network representatives, Doris Howard, is a young beautiful sexy white female computer whiz and high tech geek who agrees to work with O'Malley and Sheen.

O'Malley is attracted to Doris and smitten with her personality. He tries to impress her with his knowledge of computers and technology. She doesn't seem to be impressed. Doris asks him some sophisticated questions about computers that she knows he cannot answer, revealing that he just wants her attention. As Doris walks away from O'Malley, she whispers to him, "I strongly recommend that you keep your head on business and your other head in your pants."

"Do you have a manifest that lists which households are watching which movies?"

"No, but we have a program on our computer that we designed for billing purposes that lets us know what our customers are watching and what consumers are ordering. The computer lets us know where the movies are being broadcast, meaning what geographical location and its region. The FCC stipulates that we keep accurate billing and tracking information. We also use the numbers as a selling point for our advertisers."

Sheen pipes up, "Can your program indicate what area, neighborhood or household was watching the movie **'Outlaw Josie Wells'** about three weeks ago?"

"Let's take a look."

O'Malley is still mesmerized and checking out Doris and staring at her backside as she inputs the information on a very sophisticated key pad for a few seconds and says, "Here we go."

She prints out a long list of addresses that covers about a forty-block residential area.

O'Malley observes, "That is a lot of houses."

"That's how the program works." Doris responds.

Sheen, being pleased with a plan says, "It's a start. Thank you very much for all of your help."

The investigators leave the building with O'Malley feeling challenged by the task vocalizing, "Man, we can't cover that much ground."

"If that pretty little cookie back there was your partner you would be up with the birds trying to cover her ground."

"The early bird always catches the worm,"

"The Chief said she got the ok from the top to assign more manpower."

"We are going to need it to catch this crazy ass …"

Before he can say the "n" word, Sheen says, "Don't you even think about it."

Chapter Four
Restaurant

It is a beautiful Sunday afternoon inside a nice, upscale soul food restaurant in a high rent district. Its interior has ethnic décor, white table cloths with candle lamps and pretty flatware. The well designed restaurant with a separate wetbar holds about 100 patrons. Near the kitchen are two beautiful barmaids awaiting to greet and serve. The patrons consist mostly of middle class blacks and wealthy whites … all of whom are elegantly dressed. The men are in suits, ladies in fine dresses with matching hats. Some are dressed in African attire and their children are also neat and clean.

C.A.N. enters the restaurant. He, too, is dressed in a fine tailored Italian-made four-button pinstripe suit, blue shirt white collar and cuffs, tie and matching cuff links. He is also wearing alligator shoes, a gold diamond watch with matching rings. The doorman escorts C.A.N. to a single table in the back corner against the wall under a picture of Mary McLeod Bethune.

Melissa, a young, beautiful & sexy black waitress with big breasts, wearing a soft lovely cashmere sweater with a Historically Black College emblem brings a glass of water to C.A.N. She politely takes his order and brings him his plate of porkchops, rice and gravy and string beans.

She kindly asks, "Would you like anything else, sir?"

"Yes. I would like to have a glass of fresh milk."

"Milk, yes, the milkman brought some this morning. Large or small?"

C.A.N. says, looking at Melissa's large breasts, "Large, please."

"Whole or 2 percent?"

"All of it. Two large jugs please. I have a feeling I'm going to need them."

Melissa with a puzzled look on her face says, "I will be right back with all of your milk, sir."

While Melissa disappears into the kitchen to get the milk, a gang of four young misfits enter the restaurant. The doorman seats three at a table by the front door and the other positions himself at the bar. The misfits stay in their positions for a few minutes and then the one at the bar signals to the three at the table to go for it. The three men at the table spring to their feet, knocking over the table and everything on it. They pull out guns and yell, "Ya'll know what time it is. Give us what we come for and nobody will get hurt. After we get what we want we'll leave."

The customers are surprisingly caught off guard. A silence comes over the dinning room as they watch the misfits.

Melissa, unaware of what is going on, comes from the kitchen carrying a tray with two old fashion glass jugs full of milk. When she realizes what is going on, she tries to turn in an about face motion to go back to the kitchen. The misfit positioned at the bar by the kitchen sees Melissa with the milk jugs says, as he stares and smiles at her breast, "Where do you think you are going with those big jugs?" Melissa ignores him and tries to make her way back to the kitchen. The misfit grabs her by the arm causing her to drop the tray and spill the milk, but the jugs do not break.

C.A.N. has been watching the scene unfold the whole time. He stands up in the back of the room and yells, "You spilled my milk!"

The misfit yells back at C.A.N., "Sit your crazy ass down, nigger, less you want to die. Didn't yo mammy tell you never to cry over spilled milk?"

C.A.N. remains standing, looking crazy but not speaking. One of the other misfits who knocked over the table, walks fast toward C.A.N. with a gun in his hand yelling, "Didn't the man tell you to sit your crazy ass down? Give me your shit anyway," attempting to take C.A.N.'s, money, watch and rings. Little did he know with whom he was dealing. As he attempts to take C.A.N.'s possessions, C.A.N. grabs the man's wrist and slams his hand on the table stabbing and pinning the robber's hand to the table with a fork.

The misfits screams, "Shit!" In a quick motion, C.A.N. then elbows him in the throat while simultaneously taking his gun. C.A.N.

starts shooting at the other misfits across the room. They shoot back as customers are screaming and yelling, diving for cover, ducking under tables and crawling on the floor to safety. A big black woman wearing a big wide hat and long-haired wig gets her hat and wig shot off her head. The hat goes one way and wig flies another. Sitting at another table is an older black, semi-senile woman who remains in her seat while her family members are hiding under the table beneath the white tablecloth. The father tells his nerdy son, "Junior, get your crazy ass grandmother under the table."

Junior tries to pull his grandmother under the table but she won't go. After a few attempts, Junior finally snatches her under the table so hard that her false teeth fall out of her mouth and onto the table. The bullets flying through the room blow the teeth right off the table.

During the shootout C.A.N. kills two of the misfits leaving a third one to flee the restaurant. The fourth criminal … the one who made Melissa spill the milk gets shot in the back and falls to the floor, but is still alive. He tries to crawl to the front door. Melissa sees him trying to escape and hits him on the head with one of the milk jugs. The jug does not break because she didn't hit him hard enough as he continues to crawl towards the door. C.A.N. walks over to Melissa who is lying on the floor watching the misfit trying to crawl away. C.A.N. bends down to say to the waitress, "That's not the way you kill a thieving ass nigger like this. That's why he is still crawling. You've got to get real close and 'ba da bing." C.A.N. bashes the milk jug over the misfit's head, "So you can splatter his brain all over your nice historic black college cashmere sweater." Blood from the misfit's head splatters over Melissa and C.A.N. Melissa's eyes widen. Her face shows a strong emotion of horror. She jumps up and runs to the kitchen holding her mouth as if to throw up. The rest of the patrons are still hiding under tables, scared and crying, except for the old senile black woman who crawled from under the table and sat back in her seat.

C.A.N. walks over to the old women and says, "Grandmother you didn't eat your hoke cake" as he picks up a fork and slices off a piece and feeds it to her. The old woman with no teeth tries to eat the cake

Restaurant

he feeds her, but she spits on him. C.A.N. looks at the woman for a few seconds and says, "Them damn hoke cakes must be bad."

C.A.N. walks out of the restaurant with blood on his face, vomit and hoke cake on his clothes. As he walks out the front door Sheen and O'Malley pass him as they are running toward the restaurant. The officers briefly look at him covered in vomit and cover their mouths. Not knowing who he is, the officers turn away. With guns drawn, two other officers run into the restaurant. They rush over to the bodies lying on the floor. One policeman points a gun at one of the misfits lying on the floor. Another officer goes over to the misfit who got shot and hit with the milk jug to check his pulse, looks back at the detectives and shakes his head as to indicate the misfit is dead. By this time the restaurant is quiet with patrons still taking cover. Sheen and O'Malley look around and see all the patrons on the floor except grandma sitting at the table. The detectives try to talk to the old lady but get no response other than, "They killed my teeth."

Slowly, the patrons begin to emerge from beneath the tables and help one another up as the bartenders come from behind the bar. The room is not so quiet now because the patrons begin to chatter.

Melissa appears from the kitchen and bar area when Sheen questions her about what happened. She explains that she was returning from the kitchen to serve a customer an order of milk.

O'Malley hears this and asks, "Milk?"

"Yes, this man requested a large order of milk."

"Strange looking black man?"

"No, he was a nice looking, well-dressed brother." Sheen and O'Malley look at each other.

"Where did he go?"

"I don't know." Her voice begins to tremble as she explains to Sheen. "After he splattered that man's brains all over me and my sweater, I got sick and went into the back to clean myself up."

"Do you see him now? Is he still in the restaurant?"

"No. I believe you may have walked past him on your way in."

Sheen looking at O'Malley says, "The man covered in puke" and they both run out of the restaurant into the street to see if they can catch a glimpse of him. They return to the restaurant telling her, "He's long gone."

Melissa tells the detectives, "I believe that senior citizen over there spoke to him." O'Malley goes back to the old lady to question her. Her family explains to him that she is a little senile. O'Malley, in a calm voice tries to communicate with her anyway. "Ma'am, what did you and that man talk about? What did he say to you?"

She looks at Detective Sheen for a few seconds, opens her mouth to speak and throws up all over O'Malley. O'Malley yells, "Jesus, what the hell's wrong with that crazy ass?" and catches himself. Sheen laughs under his breath as Melissa gives O'Malley a cloth to clean himself.

As the coroners carry out the bodies and detectives leave the restaurant, O'Malley is full of anger as he cleans himself while Sheen continues to laugh. "I'm about sick and tired of chasing this crazy ass nigger around this city."

Sheen says, "I will allow you that one."

Chapter Five

CITY HALL

In a follow up meeting between Mayor Smith and Chief Stewart the Mayor shows his frustration asking, "Why haven't we caught this so-called hero? I thought by now we would've caught this fool."

"Mayor, I mean, Steve. Even though we've always been one step behind this maniac, our lead detectives have been working hard to narrow down the area where he lives. The objective is to catch him at home or not in a public place where his apprehension won't endanger the lives of innocent people."

"Have we at least found out who this fool is?"

"From the information our detectives related to the police psychologist, we've learned that this man is probably an ex-ball player, probably on steroids, which explains his agility and ability to fight and win even when the odds are stacked against him. We know that he watches a lot of TV and with the help of the network's programmers we are very close to finding him. The psychologist believes that since he only goes after bad people, he is displaying characteristics of a man who receives psychological re-enforcement of his own fears by ridding the world of evil. His allowing one victim to live in order to tell the story is an action or a message to let the world know that he does exist. But, no one can figure out or put a category on the deal with the milk. My guess is it must be a childhood issue or he's just a health nut."

"The natives are getting restless. The City council and some other groups are applying pressure on my office to catch this man. Chief, we really need to catch this fool now before he strikes again."

"We're on it, Mayor. The taskforce will start the door-to-door today."

On the street, dressed in black jackets, the taskforce goes door–to–door talking to residents about a specific black man conducting any suspicious activities. They also show the residents a police composite described by eye witness' account and a sketch drawn by the police psychologist.

As this activity is unfolding, C.A.N. enters his apartment building. He walks up the steps and into the hallway. As he puts his key in the door, he hears a noise, turns around to see a man standing at the end of the hallway in the window. The man is standing on the outside on the window ledge dressed in a dark suit. He points a gun at C.A.N.'s head and squeezes the trigger. C.A.N. hears the gun go off and sees the bullet coming from the gun and turns his head slightly but just enough away for the bullet to miss his head and hit his shoulder. The assassin stands there for a few seconds looking at C.A.N. sliding down the wall and onto the floor. The assassin lights a cigarette and disappears from sight. An elderly woman named Margret who lives down the hall from C.A.N. hears the gun go off, opens her door and sees C.A.N. in the hallway bleeding and slowly struggling to get up on his feet.

Margret walks down the hallway and tells C.A.N., "Take it easy, boy. Let me help you." She tries to help him to his feet, but fails. She stoops down and grabs C.A.N. by his ankles and drags him down the hall into her apartment leaving a slight trail of blood. Once in the apartment, she drags him back to the bedroom. She struggles to pick him up and slides him on the bed. Using pillows to elevate his feet she straps him down in the bed with belts. Margret goes into the kitchen to boil some water, sterilizing a knife and other tools needed to remove the bullet from his shoulder. Margret opens the kitchen cabinet ant gets baking soda and a plastic baggy. Gathering cloth towels, bandages and a bottle of peroxide from the bathroom linen closet she returns to the bedroom and places the wet towel on C.A.N.'s forehead. Using the sterile knife, Margret pulls the bullet out of his shoulder. He trembles and shakes, moans and groans as the bullet is being abstracted. Dr. Margret (as C.A.N sees her) then uses her needle and thread to stitch up the wound. Margret mixes the baking soda and peroxide in the plastic bag and tells him that she needs one more thing to help close those stitches and heal the wound.

C.A.N., in a weak voice says, "Milk."

Margret, "Not quite." She raises her white skirt and takes off her white underwear with a big red cross on them and squats over his shoulder where the plastic bag is and urinates over the bag. Steam and smoke rise from the bag. C.A.N., with an expression on his face that shows pain and discomfort, yells out loud in agony which echoes over the building. He breaks the straps, jumps out of the bed, knocks Margret down, runs a few steps and collapses. Margret drags him back to the bedroom, pushes him onto the bed, comforts him with soothing words while rubbing his head until he falls asleep. She covers him with sheets and a blanket and then goes into the living room and watches T.V.

The members of the taskforce continue the action of going from building to building and door-to-door looking for C.A.N. until they come to the building where he is. They enter the building and go up the steps to the second floor. They knock on the door adjacent to the one where C.A.N. and Margret are. They question the neighbor, Paul. He is a middle-aged white man (librarian type). They show Paul the composite sketch of C.A.N. Paul tells the police "I never seen that person before, but I believe there is a man that lives across the hall that is really weird, I never see his face only the back of him when he is leaving."

The lead Taskforce Office (TFO) asks, "Have you ever heard or seen anything unusual over there?"

"It is funny that you mentioned that."

"Why is that?"

"Last night I thought I heard a noise."

"A noise? What kind of noise?"

"Yeah, like a gunshot. But … when I looked out the peephole I didn't see anything."

The TFO walks across the hall and knocks on the door. There is no answer. He notices that there is dried blood on the floor in front of the door. He radios back to Sheen on his cell phone to inform him that they have found something weird. Sheen responds with a question, "Did you find the guy?"

"I'm not sure."

"What do you mean? Did you locate the suspect or not?"

"No, but we found some blood on the floor and the neighbor said he heard what he thought was a gunshot, but he didn't see anything. I think you guys might want to check this out."

Sheen and O'Malley arrive on the scene, meeting up with the taskforce officers inside the building. Sheen talking to the TFO who made the call, "Show us what you found."

"We've found what appears to be blood on the floor right here in front of this door. We think this might be the suspect's apartment."

Sheen instructs, "See if we can locate the landlord to open this door."

"Don't we need a search warrant?"

"We don't need a warrant if there is probable cause. The cause in this situation is we believe strongly there is a badly injured person inside this apartment."

They locate the landlord who is an elderly Jewish woman. Sheen explains the situation to her and she opens the door to the apartment. With their weapons drawn, the taskforce officers enter the apartment slowly and carefully with Sheen and O'Malley following behind. As they search the apartment they notice how meticulous it is but don't see anyone.

TFO speaking softly, "Maybe we've got the wrong place."

O'Malley chimes in, "I don't think so. Look at all of the T.Vs. They're in every room…even in the kitchen. Check out the refrigerator. It is full of milk." (Milk bottles are stacked neatly and in order).

The TFO in the back bedroom, standing in a walk-in closet full of suits, ties, shoes and accessories that are neatly organized says,

City Hall

"Wow, look at this closet! I have to give it to this guy, he does have good taste."

O'Malley goes into the closet and starts trying on clothes and says, "This man must do all right to be able to dress like this."

"What the hell do you think you're doing, detective? Get out of there. We might have to use that stuff for evidence. You are contaminating possible evidence – do you remember the O.J. trial?"

After O'Malley leaves the room and no one is looking, Sheen takes a nice colorful tie off the rack and slips it into his pocket. As he leaves the room, Sheen states, "It's obvious that he's not here today, but something definitely happened here."

Everyone leaves.

O'Malley asks, "If he was shot or hurt outside of his apartment and never went in his apartment, where in the hell did he go?"

"Hopefully, not far. Perhaps we need to get forensics or the blood hounds here to trace the blood trail unless someone has one of those special lights that can highlight blood stains."

The officers all look at Sheen very puzzled. Sheen recognizing their look states, "You know that light that picks up the color of blood through a special lens?"

O'Malley, "Oh yes, we learned about that in the academy. I do believe that there is one in the van. Give me the keys and I'll get it and we can shine it on the floor to see where the trail leads."

As Sheen leaves the building to retrieve the light, an older man and his dog come up the steps. As he gets to where the officers are, the dog starts to sniff and scratch around the area on the floor where C.A.N. first fell from the gun shot.

O'Malley noticing, asks, "Pops what's wrong with your mutt?"

"Nothing, he's not a mutt, he's a good boy. He's half hound dog and watch dog."

The dog with his nose to the floor begins to sniff and follow the blood scent down the hall to the door where Margret dragged C.A.N. into her apartment. The dog sniffs at her door. O'Malley signals to the other officers by waving his hands pointing down the hall for the officers to proceed down to the door. They proceed down the hall with guns drawn.

The old man asks, "What's going on fellows?"

"You and your dog go into your apartment and stay there."

The old man picks up his dog and says, "My neighbor over there is a good woman she ain't never bothered nobody."

O'Malley says to the old man, "Go into your apartment and lock your door." The old man goes inside his apartment, shuts his door and watches from the peephole.

O'Malley signals to two police officers to get on each side of Margret's door. He knocks. Margret who is watching T.V., now gets up slowly and walks to the door while still looking back at the T.V. O'Malley knocks on the door again.

Margret yells, "I'm coming. I'm coming."

The TFO whispers to O'Malley, "It sounds like an old woman." Margret answers the door in a nurse's uniform and matching hat.

O'Malley, speaking softly says to the little old lady opening the door, "Sorry to disturb you ma'am, we believe that a man we have been looking for may be in this apartment."

"What kind of man?"

"We really don't have a positive description other than this composite sketch. We do know that he is a well-dressed black man who is assumed to be armed and dangerous."

"Fool, that could be half the niggers in this city," she laughs.

"Ma'am, we need your permission to search your apartment and if the man we're looking for isn't here, we will not inconvenience you any further."

"Sorry, no need for permission. He ain't here." She tries to close her door as O'Malley signals to officers to enter the apartment. With guns drawn, the officers force their way into the apartment knocking Margret to the floor. Her hat falls off, she tumbles and hits her head hard on the floor and lies there in a semi-conscious and groggy state.

O'Malley, looking at the old woman on the floor tells one of the officers, "Stay near the front door just in case anyone tries to enter. That maniac could be anywhere."

With guns still drawn, the officers and detective look throughout the apartment. They search the living room where the TV is still on, and kitchen area where they see a make shift nurse's station, bandages and operating tools. But no sign of C.A.N. They then see the bedroom at the end of the hall. They proceed down the hall slowly with guns drawn as they enter the bedroom.

With his gun in hand, a TFO slowly approaches C.A.N. lying in bed with covers up to his neck. He nudges the man with his free hand and says, "Wake up pal, you are under arrest. You have the right to remain silent." C.A.N. doesn't respond or move. The officer shakes him again. C.A.N. remains still.

"I think he's dead." Says the TFO and signals to another TFO, Ted to check his pulse to see if he is breathing.

Ted leans over C.A.N. to see if he is breathing, then checks to see if he is dead, and says, "I can't tell."

"Pull back those covers, Ted."

Ted, already leaning over the bed attempts to pull back the covers slowly. As he pulls back the blanket C.A.N., holding a 12 gage pump shotgun next to his body fires a loud blast through the covers that sends Ted flying through the air in an upward motion toward the ceiling. The other TFO drops his gun during the blast and tries to pick it up again. C.A.N. gets out of the bed. Standing up without a shirt revealing the bandages on his shoulder, he looks at the TFO and pumps his shot gun … points it at the officer with a look on his face as if to say, 'don't even think about it.'

The TFO stops immediately in his tracks and slowly stands up and moves away from the gun that he dropped. He begins to walk backwards towards the door while keeping his eyes on C.A.N. Ted, wearing a protective vest is on the floor barely alive. The TFO scared and nervous says, "You crazy ass nigger, I'm ordering you to put down that gun before anyone else gets hurt."

C.A.N. follows the TFO slowly as he walks backward down the hall of the apartment. The officer who was told to stay near the front door is now quietly tip toeing up the hall with gun in his hand hiding behind the TFO so C.A.N. cannot see him. The TFO feels the officer's presence behind him and says to C.A.N., "Put the gun down and we can talk about this."

"I do believe y'all came here to kill me," says C.A.N.

The officer behind the TFO with gun in hand is trying to get a clean shot off to shoot C.A.N. without injuring the TFO in front of him. As the officer raises his gun over the TFO's shoulder, Margret, who is bleeding from the head from being trampled, cracks the officer over the head making a loud thump with an empty milk bottle. The hit over the head causes the officer to squeeze the trigger on his gun. The bullet enters the TFO's back knocking him to the floor. The officer who was hit with the jug turns around and shoots Margret in the chest blowing her back down the hallway. The officer has turned his back to C.A.N. and as he turns back around C.A.N. blows his head off with the shotgun.

Sheen comes back into the building, walking up the steps with a special light in his hand hears the gunshots, drops the light, runs up the steps to the area where the shots came from.

C.A.N. is now standing over Margret, sad, crying and having flash backs of his childhood of a younger woman fixing his breakfast and telling him 'don't forget to drink your milk, always drink your milk'. C.A.N. slowly walks back down the hallway crying as he pulls his shirt over his wound. The flashbacks also include a younger woman in a nurse's uniform pushing him on the swings and chasing him through the park. He and a younger Margret are walking toward a milk truck. A young, black man dressed in a white uniform sitting in the driver's seat is smiling at Margret and the little boy as they walk toward the truck. As the driver reaches out his hand to help them climb into the truck C.A.N. reaches to pull up the window and climb out of the apartment and down the fire escape to the alley.

Sheen slowly enters Margret's apartment calling for officers by name. No answers. Sheen sees the officers dead on the floor, Margret lying on the floor shot in the chest and the T.V. is still on. He goes into the kitchen and see the make shift nurse's station. On the wall he sees a picture of a young lady in a nurse's uniform holding a little boy standing next to a black man in a white milkman's uniform sitting in the milk truck. Sheen also notices that the young lady in the picture favors the old woman lying dead on the floor. He looks in the refrigerator and sees the bottles of milk.

Sheen says to himself, "Damn, this is his home where he grew up and this must be his mother. They killed his mother. Shit, things are going to get a lot worse now, for all of us." He hears a noise in the back room. He walks to the back very slowly with gun drawn and sees the window shade clanging back and forth from the wind. He looks outside the window but, C.A.N. is nowhere in sight. He goes back to the front of the apartment looks over the scene and says under his breath, "They should have waited. I don't know if we can bring him in now."

Chapter Six
ABUSE

A white man named Snooky, in his early sixties and kind of on the poor white trash side is sexually abusing a young white boy named Jimmy. Jimmy is about 10 years old and is mentally challenged or could be said to be slightly retarded. Jimmy, wearing cutoff short jeans and a t-shirt is being chased around the apartment and molested by Snooky. With continuous effort, Jimmy finally breaks free and runs crying out of the apartment down the back stairs and out of the apartment building to the alley. Too old to run, Snooky follows him down the steps running into the alley screaming, "Come back here you little son of a bitch."

Running out into the alley, Jimmy runs right into C.A.N. The physical contact knocks Jimmy to the ground and he gets up screaming in a southern dialect, "Don't let him get me. Don't let him get me."

Picking Jimmy up off the ground C.A.N. says, "You crazy ass little boy! You must be blind."

Jimmy, crying says, "Don't let him get me."

"Who? You must be having daymares, boy. I don't see nobody."

Jimmy, hanging onto C.A.N's left leg real tight says, "Over there", pointing to the sidewalk entry way to the back of the building where Snooky is now standing. "And I ain't been a dreaming. I don't dream during the daytime. He's been doing things to me."

Snooky approaches C.A.N. and says, "He's alright. He's just a little bit peculiar. When I give him his medicine, he'll be just fine."

"You crazy ass fool what have you done to this boy?"

"Just mind your own business, mister and give me back the boy."

C.A.N. stares at Jimmy and then stares at Snooky. He stares back and forth for a few seconds and asks, "This your son?"

"He's a foster child."

C.A.N. looks behind the boy and notices soil running down the back of the boy's legs. He looks up with a strange and angry expression and says, "You sick ass mother fucker, you did do something to this boy!" and begins to beat up on Snooky, using the arm and hand that aren't injured. While beating and kicking Snooky C.A.N. yells, "What kind of man would do something like that to a retarded boy?"

Jimmy shouts, "I ain't retarded! I'm mentally challenged" and bites a chunk out of Snooky's leg. Snooky screams like a stuck pig.

C.A.N., with the help of Jimmy almost beats Snooky to a pulp. C.A.N. reaches into his pocket and pulls out a pocket knife and places it at Snooky's crotch and says, "I should fix it where you can never do something like this ever again. I should cut your dick off and make you eat it."

Snooky screams out and begs for his life. C.A.N. gives the knife to Jimmy and pulls Snooky's pants down and says: "Do you have a T.V.?"

Snooky, all beat up, scared and crying says, "What the hell are you talking about?"

Jimmy responds for him, "Yeah, he has an old T.V."

"Good," C.A.N. says to Snooky, "Then you've seen the movie, '**Deliverance**'. How would you like to squeal like a pig?"

Snooky with his eyes bucked out of his head, nervous and crying says, "What the hell are you talking about?"

"I'm a man of a different kind of faith … do unto others as they have done unto others," says C.A.N. as he and Jimmy walk down the alley leaving Snooky half dead.

C.A.N. asks Jimmy, "Do you have somewhere to go?"

"No."

C.A.N. asks, "Do you have any family… somebody you can go to?"

"No."

"Well, if you're going to hang with me, we've got to get you all cleaned up and some new vines."

"Mr., can I dress up like you? Do you think it would be all right if I can get some harnesses like yours?"

"No, little nigger, you can't dress like me. And what in the hell are harnesses?"

Jimmy pointing to C.A.N.'s braces says, "Harnesses, those things holding up your britches."

"Britches, where on earth did you come from?"

"Butchers Holler."

"Who's holler? Where is that place?"

"Four days on a bus," Jimmy says.

C.A.N., looking at Jimmy says, "Damn, and I thought being black was a crime." Neighbors find Snooky in the alley half dead and call metro EMR. As EMR assists Snooky, Sheen shows up on the scene and questions him.

Sheen asks, "What happened to you? You look like you've seen a ghost."

Snooky snorts, "Worst, a nigger!"

Sheen insisted, "Just tell me what happened."

"I was walking with my boy and all of a sudden this crazy ass nig (pause) I mean a black man jumped us. And he took my boy and ran off with him."

"How old is the boy?"

"Ten."

"You seem to be a bit old to have a boy that age."

"He's a foster child and he's a little slow in the head. He's slightly retarded."

"Why do I get the feeling that you are not telling me the whole story? But for now let's try and locate the boy and get him back safe." Sheen uses his cell phone to call back to the police station and reports, "The suspect is now traveling with a boy, young white, about ten years old. They were last seen headed south in the alley behind the suspects apartment."

Sheen says to Snooky, "Let's get you to a hospital."

C.A.N. and Jimmy are now on the subway car riding toward downtown to get some fresh new clothes. As they are riding on the subway, people are looking at them strangely because of the way they look and are dressed. C.A.N. still has on his nice clothes, but its evident he has been in some kind of physical altercation and has a hurt shoulder. Jimmy is in his t-shirt and shorts. They look odd as a

Abuse

couple traveling together ... a crazy looking black man dressed well and Opie from Mayberry. Three seats up from where they are seated are three young black girls about in their early twenties. One of the girls has a little baby boy sitting on her knee. They all are playing with the baby. The girl holding the baby is bouncing the baby up and down on her knee (like a horsey ride). In the seat in front of the girls is a Wall Street, nerdy looking white man dressed in a business suit, white shirt and little bow tie reading the Wall Street Journal. As the girl, Sandy, bounces the baby up and down on her knee, he throws up and it lands on the back of the nerd's neck and it goes down his back. The girls and Jimmy laugh. The nerd jumps up from his seat, reaches for the back of his collar where the puke went down and says, "Jesus fucking Christ, can't a person sit on the subway without being used as a garbage can? What the hell's wrong with you people? Have you not any home training?"

Sandy replies, "He's just a baby. Babies do that all the time. Didn't you ever throw up when you were a baby?"

"No, not on people. If you hadn't started playing horsey with the little pick-a-ninny and feeding him junk food all the time none of this would have ever happened."

Sandy, jumps out of her seat and says, "This baby eats good all the time and who you think you calling a pick-a-ninny, you stupid ass cracker?"

"All of you! you people are all like animals. My grandfather was right, we should have never allowed you people to live in this city, urban renewal was a waste of good taxpayer's money."

Sandy approaches the nerd, gets in his face and says, "We an't no pick-a-ninnies."

Stepping toward Sandy the Nerd says: "Just sit down, girl until you get to where you are going."

"I don't have to do nothing. This is a free country. I can do whatever I want and I'm bout six seconds from kicking your ass."

The nerd retorts, "Oh yeah, I'll have all of you arrested."

Sandy laughs, "Arrested ... fool ain't no cops on this train."

"I must warn you," he adds. "I was trained in martial arts and karate in the military."

Sandy laughs, "And I'm warning you, I was trained in carazy from the hood." The argument continues to escalate. Sandy and the nerd continue to exchange words.

He steps toward Sandy when C.A.N. stands up and gives the nerd a dirty look. The nerd looks at C.A.N. and says, "You people always stick together. Why don't you mind your own business and attend to that autistic kid?"

Jimmy jumps up correcting the nerd, "I ain't autistic, I'm mentally challenged." He jumps out of his seat and attacks the man biting him on the leg. Mr. nerdy Wall Street kicks Jimmy off his leg and he stumbles backward and falls into C.A.N. C.A.N. helps Jimmy up off the floor and Jimmy goes back after the nerd again. C.A.N. is smiling at this point as he watches Sandy, Jimmy and the nerd battle. The scuffle goes on for about a minute, but they can't get the nerd down. He is a tough little bastard. Mr. Nerd pulls an ink pen out of his jacket pocket and attempts to stab at the other girls who joined in the commotion.

Sandy quips, "So you want to use weapons." C.A.N. snatches the pen out of the nerd's hand and puts him in a headlock while the girls beat him with their cell phones and purses.

One of the girls, Latisha says, "Oh lord. you done made me break my Gucci bag." as she hits the nerd over the head with the bag. Jimmy bites the nerd's ear.

He screams out loud and C.A.N. lets him out of the headlock. The nerd falls to the floor holding his ear, blood running down his face, trembling and shaking says, "All of you niggers are crazy!"

C.A.N. says to Jimmy, "You did have a T.V. You been watching Mike Tyson?" C.A.N., Jimmy and the girls get off at the next stop leaving the nerd on the subway car. The two girls and the baby go their separate ways and Sandy follows C.A.N. and Jimmy. C.A.N. tells Sandy, "Shouldn't you be going with your girl friends?"

Sandy does not answer she just looks at him and smiles.

C.A.N. turns to Sandy asking, "You trying to hang with us?"

"I think I'll be cool with y'all because I know that man back there is going to send the police to come after us for what we did. He deserved it, talking to us like that. He lucky we didn't kill'em. Where are we going anyway?"

"We are going to get some new clothes, and I'm going to get some braces".

"Braces, you mean for your teeth?"

"No, for my new britches".

Sandy looking at C.A.N. says, "What is that little cracker talking about?" C.A.N. points to and pulls up on his braces connected to his pants.

"Oh, ya'll talking bout gettin hooked, with some silks. You must know some Italians."

Chapter Seven
HOSPITAL

Sheen is at the hospital in the emergency room with Snooky. A doctor and two female nurses, one white and the other Asian are examining Snooky while Sheen continues to question him about the incident. The doctor, a black man is concerned about the bite marks. The doctor examining the teeth marks asks "Where did these bite marks come from?"

"From the kid, I think."

Doctor (smiling) smirks, "This kid must have been awful hungry to bite you like this."

Sheen, looking suspicious at Snooky, "If the boy was a foster child living with you why in the hell would he bite you like that? What did you do to him for him to turn on you?"

"I don't know, like I told you, the boy is retarded. When he doesn't have his medicine, it's no telling what he will do."

While Sheen is in the emergency room talking to Snooky and the doctors, the nerd has been admitted to the emergency room and is being escorted by doctors back to the section next to where they are. Sheen hears the nerd telling the doctors, "As I was riding on the subway, a crazy black man, with a little retarded white boy and a group of crazy black girls ganged up on me. The boy tried to bite off my ear!"

Sheen goes over to where the nerd is being examined by a doctor and introduces himself to the nerd and asked him, "Could you please give me a description of this black man?"

As Sheen and the nerd discuss the details of the subway incident, the doctor interrupts the conversation and says: "We have some information that just may interest you."

Sheen excuses himself from the nerd and ask the doctor, "Concerning?"

"Concerning our patient, Snooky and gives Sheen a medical report case file and explains to him, "That boy was admitted to the hospital and treated for what was believed to be sexual abuse. At the time of the alleged incident the boy was under foster care. We reported the situation to the social services, and police were called in. Please do not let anyone know I showed you this report or that we had this conversation because of Hippa, the Patient Privacy Act, I could lose my job."

"I understand and I will keep it confidential. But tell me what happened to the case."

"When the hospital encounters situations that seems suspect or criminal, we are only required by law to inform the authorities."

"Did you all follow up on the case."

"We don't follow up because we don't have the legal power to investigate the crime, prosecute the alleged accused or represent the victim. After we inform the authorities, we are no longer involved unless we are summoned to testify or are implicated through the medical services provided by the hospital. Besides, the Lord works in mysterious ways."

"You know my mother drilled that in my head a million times, and I never understood it. I don't know what you mean by that. What does it have to do with this situation?"

"You are here, aren't you?"

Sheen looks at the doctor for a few seconds and then the light bulb goes on in his head. He goes back to where Snooky is and tells the doctors, "I need to speak to this man alone." They leave the room.

Sheen, speaking to Snooky with anger in his voice, "You piece of shit. I now know why that man kick the shit out of you. He only retaliates in revenge for who he feels are innocent. You abused that retarded boy and the man must have seen it or found out about it somehow."

Snooky, sitting on the table all bandaged up says, "I didn't do that and you have no proof I did."

"Don't insult my intelligence. I know what you did and so do other people. Because of budget cuts and staff shortages, the system didn't pursue the case. Somehow that man found out about what you did to that boy. You are damn lucky he didn't kill you like he did the rest of his victims. You molesting ass cracker. I should run you in myself, but I don't have time for that now. I've got to find them because there are people out there who are going to try and kill that man and that boy might get killed just by being with him. According to the latest survivor, some girl has joined them and she could also end up being a tragedy."

It's Friday morning. C.A.N., Jimmy and Sandy are walking down the street in brand new clothes and dressed very well, one might add. C.A.N. has on a navy blue pin stripped suit, a dress blue shirt with white collar and white French cuffs, blue and white cuff links, a flashy silk tie with matching braces, blue and white crocodile shoes and his signature glass pipe around his neck. Jimmy is dressed the same way (smaller version of the C.A.N) with a glass whistle around his neck. Sandy is dressed in an expensive female version of a pin stripped dress suit, white shirt, open collar, cuffs showing, stockings, Ferragamo shoes and professional business hair style … non-ghetto fabulous with a glass pipe around her neck. They are walking together side by side down the street at a fast-paced stroll. Jimmy has to take double steps in order to keep up. As they stroll they turn up bottles of milk to their mouths in sync drinking their milk while walking like soldiers marching in a parade. They stroll right pass city hall where the Mayor and the Chief are having another conversation while they are drinking their coffee.

Mayor Smith shares some insight. "It has been brought to my attention that our suspect has gone from fool to public menace and is still performing. I understand, now, with added attractions.

"Yeah, Mayor. According to my lead detective, Sheen, it appears that he saved a little retarded boy from an abusive foster parent. The maniac and the boy really worked this old white man over pretty good. The boy almost chewed the old man to death."

"We don't want the press to get a hold of that story. This maniac will have a bigger following. What about this young black girl?"

"Apparently, there was some sort of altercation on the subway car that the suspect and boy were riding."

"Altercation? I heard it was almost a race riot."

"A riot, as in a comedy act. Sheen interviewed the victim at the hospital who claims a baby that a woman was holding in her lap threw up on him."

Mayor Smith, smiling, "Threw up on him?"

Chief Stewart returning the smile, "Yes, down his back."

Mayor Smith, now laughing, says, "That must have been awful."

Oh, It gets better, Mayor. The victim got upset and started using racial overtones at the girls on the subway who then got angry at his tones and jumped him right on the subway.

"My god! Were there any weapons involved?"

"Yes, as a matter of fact," the Chief laughs …"cell phones and purses. They clobbered the victim with modern technology and Gucci bags."

They are both laughing out loud at this point.

Chief Stewart hypothesizes, "It is my guess that one of the young girls must have left with the maniac and the little retarded boy. The victim also said that the boy tried to bite his ear off."

"Chief, this is getting way out of hand. Are we any closer to finding out who this maniac is?"

"Yes, we pulled blood samples from the crime scene. The blood from the bed in that apartment tested negative for drugs, but positive for steroids."

"I was told that he carries a crack pipe around his neck."

"He does, but he's not smoking crack. Apparently, it must be something else".

"Is it possible to smoke steroids?""

No, but we traced the type of steroids back to a pharmaceutical outfit that informed us that it was a brand that is highly used by professional athletes. This leads us to believe that he is an athlete … maybe an ex-ballplayer of some type. Also, the surviving witnesses said that he speaks with a southern accent."

"Steroids, isn't that stuff illegal or at least considered an illegal substance? I remember how that stuff ruined my brother's son who was on the college wrestling team."

"Well, Mayor, our people in the crime lab stated that what he was smoking was of a milk substance."

"Milk? How on earth do you smoke milk?"

"Again, according to our people in the lab, he has found a way to transform the milk into a rock substance like crack and is able to smoke it. This man is really crazy!"

Okay, Chief, let's get back to the business at hand. This fool continues to gain support from sympathizers and victims who feel that their cries go unheard. And he is smoking milk!"

"Yeah, if that don't beat all. My husband who hasn't seen much of me lately, especially since this whole thing started, had the nerve to buy one of those dam T-shirts. I believe he did it just to piss me off."

"Like I said, he's gaining more moral support for going after and hurting the bad guys."

"Bad guys my ass, those officers under my command were not bad guys."

"Are you sure about that Chief?"

"To my knowledge, yes! What are you trying to say, Mayor? Do you know something I don't? Say it!"

"All I am saying, Chief, is check your back door.

"You mean to tell me that there are members on my team going behind my back, going out on their own?"

"My sources tell me that there is a bounty, meaning an initiative to neutralize this fool and the cooperative came from within, your department."

"Mayor, if I may be so bold, I believe you may be fishing in the wrong pond."

"Didn't you say that you had your best detectives handling the situation?"

"Yes, one of our taskforce officers was killed by that maniac."

"Where was the lead detective?"

After a long pause, Sally responds curtly "He left the detectives and the taskforce officers in the building while he went to retrieve a piece of equipment to trace the blood they found on the floor in the hallway."

"So your lead detective did not see, hear or witness what transpired between the officers and the fool? Therefore, we don't have a true picture of how the officers and the old lady were killed. If my experience and memory serves me correctly, those officers should not have entered that apartment without the lead detective or additional back up."

"They probably felt that they had just cause to enter the apartment because a suspected criminal and/or an injured person were inside."

"Chief, doesn't that strike you as being a little odd?"

"What, that they went the extra mile to catch this maniac?"

"No, that they tried to kill him?"

"I am not following you."

"If the story is correct and the man was injured and lying in the bed, wouldn't that create an opportunity for the officers to put the cuffs on him?" Chief Stewart does not answer.

"Let me say it again, Chief, and please forgive me for being repetitive, bring this fool in to stand trial so that the public can see that law enforcement in my city still works. And for us to send a message to everyone that they cannot take matters into their own hands, even with public support and I'm sick of looking at those damn T-shirts!"

Chapter Eight

HEADQUARTERS

Back at headquarters, Chief Stewart is now having a conversation with Sheen as she states emphatically, "We have got to catch this maniac, and I mean now."

"Chief, we can get him now because he has made our job a little easier with the crew that's now traveling with him. He won't be able to move so swiftly with that retarded boy and crazy hoochie momma. Incognito, he cannot be."

"This crazy behavior that he has been demonstrating, it's like he is toying with us. He's got to know that those people will slow him down. Why would they follow a crazy man like that around the city, knowing that it could get them in trouble or even killed?"

"The boy probably doesn't know what is going on, the girl must be just as crazy as he is, she's probably a crack head."

"It is an unusual set of circumstances that's for sure. Say, there is something else I need to discuss with you. I need you to tell it to me straight. Is any one of our guys working with you on this case on the take?"

"Some of our guys may shake out a few nickels and dimes from bad guys, especially from drug dealers, but I can't see it in this case. This maniac is not really connected to anything but madness, so I really don't see why one of our officers would. I don't see a logical reason or benefit."

"They may see it as beneficial, but it's never logical."

"Chief, you must have heard something."

"Just keep your ears open and watch your back."

Sheen, feeling disrespected and looking puzzled says, "Are we finished here?"

"You're excused. There is one more thing, catch him alive if you can. There needs to be a trial."

Sheen says under his breath as he is walking out the door, "Trial, yeah, give the public another reason to love this crazy ass nigger."

Leaving the building and walking down the street he is approached by a welldressed white man, a business type (looks like a wealthy lawyer) who walks down the street with Sheen and introduces himself as Jack Hamilton and asks, "How is the investigation coming along?"

"I am not talking to the press, and I don't want to be on your T.V. show. You all make him look like some sort of a hero and that it ain't right."

Hamilton responds, "I'm not from the press and he is a long way from being a John Wayne."

"What organization or special interest group do you represent?"

"If you allow me a few minutes of your time to elucidate the position of my interest."

Sheen, laughing asks, "Elu a who?"

"Detective?"

"That's lead detective."

"Excuse me, lead detective. Let me explain the reason why I requested your time. The interest that I represent insists on having our problem eradicated."

"I have orders to bring this man in so that he can be prosecuted," Sheen told Hamilton.

Hamilton tries to hand Sheen a regular sized white envelope (full of money). Sheen (refusing to take the envelope) says, "I don't sleep with the devil, therefore, nobody owns my soul."

"We don't care who you sleep with … we just want the problem resolved."

"I don't care how many bad guys he erases, I will bring him in, you can bet on it. And I will personally make sure he stands trial, especially for what he did to my partner."

"It seems that we have something in common."

"We do? What could that possibly be?"

"Listen carefully, my friend, we visited your partner in the market place. He sold us a bill of goods that he didn't deliver on."

"I don't believe that! My partner wasn't a shopper. He was young and a little on the wild side but he wasn't that stupid."

"We are not interested in your beliefs lead detective."

"Like I said, I have my orders. Besides, it seems that ya'll made an attempt to purchase your own goods and tried to use my partner to ensure that the package got delivered. And now you're back with your receipt trying to get re-reimbursed. Sorry, store policy is no returns, no refunds and no exchanges." Hamilton stands there silent with the envelope in his hands as Sheen walks away.

Chapter Nine

STAKEOUT

Sheen and the taskforce officers are in plain clothes sitting in unmarked cars staking out C.A.N.'s apartment building. The taskforce watches as C.A.N., Jimmy and Sandy enter the building wearing their nice clothes, resembling professional business people. One of the TFO states, "They look too good to be criminals."

TFO asks Sheen, "What are we waiting for? Let's get them."

"They are not going anywhere. Let them get settled and comfortable. Plus, we can use the element of surprise in our favor."

C.A.N. and Jimmy are in the living room area sitting on the couch drinking milk and watching T.V. while Sandy is in the kitchen cooking food, singing, dancing and prancing around. Sandy slips and falls in the kitchen. C.A.N. hears her fall and goes in the kitchen and sees her on the floor laughing from her fall. He picks her up off the floor as she looks into his eyes with lust, and she puts her arms around his neck, hugs and kisses him.

C.A.N. asks, "How old are you?"

"Twenty-four. Why? You don't want to get busy with me, do ya?"

C.A.N. and Sandy are now hugging and kissing, getting very passionate and sexual. C.A.N. begins to help Sandy undress as she takes her pants with one hand and helps him take off his pants with her other hand. The couple are making hot steamy love on the kitchen counter top where heavy breathing and hard stroking is choreographed. As they are stroking, a full bottle of milk that was on the counter begins to shake, tipping back and forth before and about to fall off the counter. C.A.N. catches the bottle with his foot, kicks it up in the air and catches it with his hand without spilling a drop and drinks the milk without skipping a stroke. Going at it pretty heavily, they are not aware that Jimmy appears out of nowhere, standing there with s strange look on his face as he watches them having wild and crazy sex. As Jimmy watches this activity, he has flashbacks of being abused by Snooky.

Sandy looks down and sees Jimmy staring up at them, taps C.A.N. on his shoulder and points to Jimmy. C.A.N. turns around and sees Jimmy standing there with a strange teary eyed facial expression. C.A.N. and Sandy stop their activity and look at Jimmy in a way that suggest 'go away little boy.'

The TFO officers are now coming up the hall. Sheen whispers to the officers, "Gentlemen, we've been here before. Be very careful. This guy can slide between the molecules of wetness like an eel through seaweed. We have orders to take this man alive. Try to remember that."

As C.A.N. and Sandy stop to look at Jimmy, there is a knock at the door. The apartment is quiet. Sheen knocks again. C.A.N and Sandy are still in their sexual positions with her legs wrapped around his waist while he is standing up straight. Jimmy is standing beside C.A.N. C.A.N. signals to Sandy to answer the door.

Sandy, still in the same position yells, "Who is it?"

"It's the police ma'am. We have a search warrant, but I just want to talk to you if I could please."

Sandy, wearing nothing but a long sleeve white dress shirt is helped down off the countertop by CA.N. who signals to her to open the refrigerator. She obeys his request. He gives further instructions to both Sandy and Jimmy to take the bottles of milk out and pour on the floor, down the hall and spread it in front of the doorway where the police are.

"Ma'am, are you there, please open the door." C.A.N. signals to Sandy to stall them.

"Yes, wait a minute. I need to put some clothes on."

C.A.N. quickly but quietly rips the electrical cords from the toaster, microwave and other appliances. He gets a knife from a kitchen cabinet drawer, cuts and peels the rubber off the cords and then raps and ties the cords together and places them in the milk and plugs the cords into an electrical outlet. Watching this activity, Sandy and Jimmy look puzzled and confused as they try to figure out what C.A.N. is doing. They are also amazed at his swiftness.

Sheen says to the officers, "Something is wrong. She is taking too long," as he signals to the officers to pull their weapons. With Sheen behind them, the officers pull their weapons and kick the door in. The medal door falls on the milk with the powerful electric current running through it. A loud electrical explosion occurs. The officers are blown back and out of the apartment and into Sheen. They are thrown against and through the door of the apartment across the hall landing in that living room. They land in the living room of the old white man who had the sniffing dog. He is sitting in his living room wearing one of those Milk Man T-shirts. The officers and Sheen are lying on the floor groggy, dazed and confused trying to figure out what happened.

Getting up slowly from the floor, one of the officers asks, "What the hell just happened?"

The old white man with his dog sitting at his feet says, "Ya'll been over there fucking with that crazy ass nigger, weren't ja? I just want to know who's going to fix my door?"

Chapter Ten

THE CHASE

During the explosion, the crew of C.A.N., Jimmy and Sandy escape from the apartment through the window in the back bedroom. Fire and smoke fill the front of the apartment as they make their escape. The crew climbs over the balcony and down the fire escape ladder. C.A.N. helps the other two off and down to the ground. They walk fast down the alley as C.A.N and Sandy hold Jimmy's hand so he can keep up. C.A.N. still has his pipe around his neck and Jimmy still has his whistle around his. They can hear police and emergency sirens from a distance, the sirens become louder as they walk down the alley. As they walk further down the alley, they can hear a James Brown song playing at a close distance. Sandy sees an older black man detailing an older model Dodge Charger (Hemi) in mint condition, chrome wheels and spoiler on the trunk. The James Brown song is coming from that car. Sandy taps C.A.N. on the shoulder and points to the black man detailing his car and listening to James Brown. C.A.N. signals to Sandy to go over there and deal with the man. Sandy, looking young and sexy in the dress shirt goes over and gets real close to the man and says, "Hey, pops."

Pops, who is down shinning the tires, gets a close up look right up at Sandy's crotch says, with a big smile on his face, "Yes, darling, what in God's name can I do for a pretty young sexy thing like you?"

"How about taking me for a ride in this old jalopy?"

"She ain't no jalopy. She's a classic, the last of it's kind and she can run!"

"Oh yeah?"

"Oh yeah, she can make a snake and show 'em how to crawl."

As Sandy and Pops converse, his back is turned to the car and the rest of the crew. While Sandy stands close to him, CA.N and Jimmy creep up along the other side of the car. C.A.N eases in the driver's seat while Jimmy slides quietly into the back seat. C.A.N. starts the car, it kicks off with a loud glass pack muffler sound with a fine tuned engine.

Pops turns around and says, "What the hell is going on here?"

The car pulls off. Sandy runs alongside of the car with Jimmy laughing like it's a game and says, "Jump, come on, jump." Sandy quickly jumps in and the car drives off down the alley.

Pops, watching the car drive away, slams his detailing rag on the ground and says, "If that don't beat all? My wife always said sniffing around that young pussy would be my downfall. I'll kiss a fat baby's butt."

The Chase

The Crew turns out from the alley and onto the street. As they turn onto the street, they see the police cars and ambulances back at the apartment building. Sheen is being attended to by paramedics, hears the sound of the car, looks up and sees Jimmy in the back seat who is looking back at the flashing lights. Sheen recognizes Jimmy from the photo in the report shown to him by the doctors at the hospital. Sheen, all bruised up gets up immediately, limps away from the paramedics, gets into to his unmarked car and chases the crew. As he gets closer to the crew, Sandy looks at Jimmy in the back seat asking, "What you looking at back there?" Jimmy doesn't answer. Sandy sees Sheen in the unmarked car and taps C.A.N. on his shoulder and says, "Don't look now, but I think we have company." He looks in the mirror, sees Sheen's face and a quick flash back of seeing Sheen's face as he was climbing out the window after the taskforce officers killed his mother. C.A.N signals to Jimmy and Sandy to buckle up. C.A.N. steps on the gas and Sheen gives chase.

The chase ends up being an eight-minute wild ride through the streets. Sandy is scared from the fast and dangerous pace as C.A.N is shifting gears, whipping around corners and flying over bumps in the road. As he is whipping around corners and flying over the bumps, Jimmy is sliding across the back seat and jumping up and down, smiling and laughing as he is enjoying the ride … the roller coaster ride. Sheen is doing a pretty good job keeping up with the C.A.N. They both display exceptional driving skills, until Sheen swerves to avoid a woman pushing a baby carriage. He wipes out and his car flips over and catches fire. C.A.N. stops his car, puts it in reverse and backs up to Sheen. As the car is burning, C.A.N. pulls Sheen out of the car who is still alive. Sandy and Jimmy observe what he is going on, but are unsure what C.A.N.'s intentions are. Sheen is lying on the street hurt and dazed thinking that C.A.N. is going to kill him and he slowly reaches for his gun. C.A.N. stares into Sheen's eyes for a few seconds, Sheen stares back into C.A.N. eyes and then removes his hand from his gun. Sheen, looking up at the crew with a faint and weak voice says: "Who are you people?"

Jimmy answers, "We are middle class Negroes. We get our proper nourishment every day and we drink our milk." C.A.N gives Sheen a hit off the pipe and signals to Jimmy who gives Sheen a sip of milk. The Crew walks away and gets back into the car. Sheen, still lying on the street watches the crew drive off into the distance.

As the crew drives away C.A.N torts, "We are out of milk."

Sandy smiles, slides across the seat and sits close to him, opens up her shirt and shows him her breast and says, "I've got milk." C.A.N does not look at Sandy and pushes her away.

"You must keep your eyes on the road at all times," Jimmy coaches from the back seat.

Sandy, closing her shirt as she slides back over to her side of the car says, "We can't be riding in this car all day. They are going to be looking for us. We got to find a place to go. We need to find a new place to stay."

"Yea, a place that has milk," C.A.N. agrees.

"With a T.V. with color, a flat screen," Jimmy adds.

Sandy chimes in, "And with a soft bed."

They turn onto a street that is in an upper class neighborhood known as Chevy Chase lined with big beautiful houses and meticulously manicured lawns.

"I know all of these houses got T.V's but how you going to know which of these houses got milk in the refrigerator?" questions Sandy.

C.A.N. pulls in a long driveway up into the garage of a big nice house. Sandy and Jimmy look at him very strangely. He gets out of the car and shuts the door. Sandy and Jimmy are still sitting in the car watching him as he walks over to the entrance, punches in a code on the alarm key pad unlocking the door. He looks back at them and says, "What y'all waiting for? Lets go." They get out of the car and follow him into the house and the garage door closes behind them. As they stroll through the house, Sandy and Jimmy notice the beautiful décor, color scheme and nice furniture. C.A.N. goes straight to the kitchen to the refrigerator and gets a bottle of milk. As he is drinking the milk he notices through the kitchen window a white utility van with a plumbing repair logo on the panel drive slowly by as if to be looking for an address or casing the neighborhood. Inside the vehicle are three white men and one white girl, all dressed in work uniforms. While C.A.N. studies this scene, Jimmy goes into the family room next to the kitchen area and turns on the T.V, sits down on the couch and watches T.V. C.A.N pulls out cold cuts and condiments from the frig and makes sandwiches.

Sandy goes into a room that seem to be a den, library or sports room where the walls are adorned with pictures and plaques along with several trophies and sports memorabilia filling the room. Sandy also notices a picture on the stand of a young white couple standing together with a young black female dressed in a nurse'a uniform and hat holding a little white baby in her arms with a little black boy standing next to her holding onto her leg. Sandy takes a real good look at the picture and notices that the white man is also in most of the other pictures on the wall. She also notices that the young black woman in the picture looks like a older version of the black woman that she saw in a picture back at C.A.N.'s apartment. And that the little boy favors the milkman in the picture. While she studies the pictures, C.A.N. takes a tray of sandwiches and milk into the family area where Jimmy is watching T.V. Sandy comes into the room and joins them on the couch. She stares at C.A.N. with a the look of a thousand questions. They eat their sandwiches while watching the movie, **'Magnum Force'** where Eastwood says, "A man's got to know his limitations."

With the remote, Jimmy turns the channel to Dirty Harry. He turns the channel again and Eastwood says, "I know what you're thinking punk ... did he shoot six rounds or just five? You'll have to ask yourself one question, do you feel lucky, punk?"

Sandy spouts, "I seen these movies when I was little. My father used to watch them all the time."

Jimmy continues to flip through channels and stops on the movie, **'Scar Face'** at the scene where Al Pacino screams, "Say hello to my little friend." Again, Sandy says, "I've seen this movie too. We missed the part where they saw that man up in the bathtub."

The crew finishes their lunches and continues to watch T.V. until they all get kind of drowsy and Sandy falls asleep. As she dozes, The Andy Griffith show comes on with the whistling tune with Andy and Opie walking to the creek to go fishing. Hearing the tune Sandy wakes up.

Jimmy says, "I used to go fishing with my real fatha all the time before he died.

"I hated fishing cause my father used to make us clean 'em after he chopped the heads off. And those catfish, (reaching up toward her upper lip area like she has mustache whiskers) with those little whiskers, they were nasty," sneered Sandy.

C.A.N., speaking to Jimmy, "How did you lose your father?"

"I didn't lose him. He died. He got all hurt up … real bad down at the mill."

C.A.N. then asked, "What happened to your mother?"

"After my fatha got hurt she tooken left and grandma died and the church sent me up here to live with Snooky that you tooken whupped up on."

Jimmy turns to C.A.N. and asks, "Did you ever have a fatha?"

C.A.N becomes very quiet, his face begins to drop and an expression of sadness over comes him. He has a flashback going back 20 years of being in the same neighborhood. In this flash, there is an older style milk truck (same milk truck as in the previous photos on the wall). A black boy is peddling on a little bicycle down a sidewalk at the same speed as the milk truck. The driver is looking at the boy with his hands tightly on the steering wheel pretending to be racing the boy. The boy is looking at the driver. They are smiling at each other as the driver continues to pretend racing the boy as the boy displays an expression of determination on his face and in his body language as he peddles harder to keep up with the milk truck. The little boy says to his competition, "I'm going to beat you this time daddy," as he peddles faster picking up speed. The truck is cruising slower so the boy can appear to be winning the race. The little one is now huffing and puffing as he peddles faster getting ahead of the truck. The driver has an expression of joy and pleasure watching his son trying so hard to win. The driver is pleased with the determination and effort of his son trying to win. The little one is really trying to impress his father with his ability to ride and his athleticism to keep up. They race on toward the intersection. As they race towards the intersection, a big black four door sedan pulls across the intersection (four way stop light) as the traffic light facing the truck turns red, the truck and car come to a stop. The doors on the passenger's side of the car open at the same time and two white men wearing dark glasses, nice dark suits with white shirts step out of the vehicle with machine guns. The boy does not see the car stop and the men get out because he is still watching the truck when the two men fire their guns spraying the truck with bullets. The bullets hit the front of the truck's grill and windshield. Now the boy watches the bullets as they fly through the windshield. The windshield cracks, falls apart and glass flies everywhere. As the bullets fly into the truck they crack and burst the bottles spilling milk all over the floor. The Boy watches as bullets hit the driver in the face and neck, bullets rip the driver's chest open and blood pours out of his chest and all over his white uniform, his bowtie falls off. His eyes almost grow out of his head as he watches this terrible and horrifying scene. The driver finally falls forward and slumps over the steering wheel as the truck rolls toward the men in the black car. One of the gunmen shoots out the tires of the truck to stop its momentum from rolling forward toward them. The truck crawls to a slow halt. The gunman that got out of the front passenger door says: "That will send a message, nobody rides our routes without paying. I don't know why that nigger thought he could. He must be crazy!"

Laughing, the other gunman says, "Because he is a crazy ass nigger that's why. The nigger delivers no more." The gunmen get back into the car and drive away. The boy stands on the sidewalk with his bicycle between his legs and a look of terror on his face. He is frozen stiff, eyes and mouth wide open and tears rolling down his face. Blood is dripping down the steering wheel of the truck from where the driver has slumped over. Blood is also dripping down the steps of the entryway on the truck and onto the pavement. The blood from the driver turns a Pepto Bismol pink as it mixes with the milk that exploded from the broken bottles. The boy watches as the pink color of blood run down the steps of the truck and onto the pavement.

Still in part of the flashback state, C.A.N. remembers suddenly two white arms scoop the boy off the bicycle. It is a younger looking white woman, dressed very well who picks the boy up into her arms and carries him away from the scene and into a house nearby. (Unknown to the Crew, it is the house they are currently visiting). As the woman carries the boy into the house they are met by a welldressed white man wearing an ascot around his neck. With a British accent the man says, "Dear God, Martha, what on earth is going on? I was out on the veranda writing in my ledger when I heard what sounded like gunfire. Why are you carrying the little chap? Is he injured?"

"Henry, come quickly. Henry, something terrible has happened. Call the authorities."

Henry, taking the boy from Martha's arms asks, "For heaven's sake, what has this little chap done?"

Martha, as she picks up the phone to call the authorities, surmises, "I believe he was following the milk truck when a robbery occurred."

Carrying the little boy to the room by the kitchen, in a puzzled tone, Henry asked, "Robbery, dear heavens, in this neighborhood?"

"Yes Henry. These men with guns shot up the milk truck. It was awful. Check the boy, Henry. Make sure he is not harmed. Those bullets were soaring everywhere."

Henry looking over the little boy for injuries says, "This is odd, this boy is colored."

"What is so odd about that?"

"I haven't seen many coloreds in this neighborhood. He doesn't appear to be injured."

"He is a just a little boy Henry, it doesn't matter."

"I know that Martha, it's just unusual around here that's all."

"Fonse retired a few months ago and moved to Florida with his new wife. That's why we have a new man, you know there is a Negro fellow delivering the milk and dairy products now. There is no way anyone could have possibly survived that awful robbery."

"Old Fonse retired?"

"Yes Henry, a few months now".

Henry looking into the little boy's eyes asked him, "What is your name, mate?" The little boy doesn't answer.

"This mate is scared speechless."

"He witnessed the robbery."

"What on earth is he doing in this neighborhood? Why was he following the milk truck?"

"He must have known the new milkman."

Martha sitting down beside the little boy asks softly, "Son, did you know the milkman? Was he a friend of yours? Was he a relative?" No answer.

"He must be in shock."

"We will turn him over to the authorities when they arrive."

"We will do no such thing!"

"For Heavens sake, Martha, what are you babbling on about?"

"He will stay here with us. We will nurse him until he is able to speak and then we will learn his name and contact his family."

"Can't we just let the authorities handle it? They will know what to do. They are trained for this type of thing."

"Oh Henry, only God knows what they will do with him. You know how they treat Negroes. For now this will be his home until we locate his biological family." C.A.N. comes back to the present ending his flashback.

C.A.N's eyes filled with tears as he realizes he is sitting in the same spot in the same room when he was there as a little boy sitting next to Martha and Henry.

Chapter Eleven

HOUSE CRASHERS

Looking at the house where the Crew is, the driver of the work van, Sony, says, "This place looks just as good as any."

His partner, Jose, sitting on the passenger's side responds with, "A house like that should have a lot of goodies."

Malik, the third man sitting in the back next to Susie chimes in with, "Let's hope so folks, because that last house was worthless, a bunch of worthless antiques."

From the back seat, Susie agrees. "I know, right. You wouldn't think that these kind of people would hang on to a bunch of old worthless shit."

"Those antiques was good stuff. We just didn't have time to get rid of it," Sony declares.

"This house should have a lot of nice pretty things a pretty girl like me can keep or sell."

"We have to sell this heist. I got a buyer for the good stuff." backing the van into to the driveway.

The crew inside the house doesn't see or hear the van because they are asleep. The gang gets out of the van with tool bags looking like repair workers. They ring the doorbell. The doorbell rings softly. The crew inside are still on the couch sprawled out sleeping. The volume on the T.V. prevents them from hearing the soft doorbell ring. No one answers the door. The gang outside decides to use their work tools to pick the locks on the front door and they enter the house.

Sandy, sleeping on the couch with her head resting on C.A.N.'s shoulder, thinks she hears something, looks up and does not see anything goes back to sleep. She hears a second noise and wakes up to see what it is. She is startled when she meets the gang in the hallway. Thinking on her feet as she sees the gang dressed in repair uniforms, Sandy says, "I'm the maid. Can I help you?"

Sony, with a quick response, "We are with the gas company ma'am and we are here to check your gas line. Our computer back at headquarters indicated there is a gas leak in this area. We were ordered to investigate it. I believe your door was unlocked."

"I am just the maid. Y 'all have to come back when the Mr. and the Mrs. are here." Thinking that she is alone, the crew bum rush Sandy. They drag her from the hall way into the first room on the right. The other two men attempt to sexually assault her.

"Keep your dicks in your pants and do what we came here for," orders Susie. Let's get the shit and go".

"Jealous because we ain't trying to get busy with you?"

"Whatever," and she leaves the room.

Sony peeps his head in the room and says, "Have fun boys."

The two men carry Sandy into another room and begin tearing her clothes off. Sandy is fighting back with all her might, kicking and swinging and says, "Y 'all are gonna to have to kill me first. Wait to my man comes."

Jose, "Right now you are home alone Aunt Jemima and we'll be done and gone by the time Bojangles gets home." Both men laugh.

C.A.N., knowing the layout of the house sneaks up stairs and Jimmy follows. They make their way upstairs to the master bedroom's walk-in closet where there is a fancy gun collection. C.A.N. breaks the lock off door to get into the gun closet. He takes a few guns and hands a gun to Jimmy. He whispers to Jimmy, "Do you know how to use one of these?"

"Yes, my real fatha taught it to me and I saw it in those movies."

C.A.N. looks at Jimmy and says, "Shit."

Downstairs Sandy's clothes are torn off and as Jose is about to penetrate her, she looks up with a big smile on her face. Jose asked,

"Whatcha smiling at Aunt Jemima? You beginning to enjoy this? You girls like it rough don't cha?"

Feeling something strange, the two men turn around and see C.A.N standing there by himself and Jose ask him, "Where'd the hell did you come from? We cased this place first. Go find your own house to take down."

C.A.N. remains calm and quiet and doesn't answer.

"If you want this bitch you are going to have to wait your turn."

C.A.N, with pipe around his neck takes a hit and says loudly, "Get away from her, now!"

"You share some of that good shit you're smoking and you can have this bitch."

C.A.N. yells again, "Let her go!"

Malik, feeling pretty sure of himself quips, "He's by himself. Get that crazy ass nigger."

As Malik takes a step toward C.A.N., C.A.N. screams, "Say hello to my little friend," as Jimmy jumps from behind him with a gun almost bigger than he is and shoots Malik in the chest blowing him backwards into the wall knocking pictures and other items off the wall. Hearing the blast, Jose lets Sandy go while she puts her tattered clothes back on and runs for cover. Jose, who is now terrified and scared to death, is trembling, unable to speak and is frozen in place.

Jimmy, looking at Jose with a blank look on his face says, "I know what you are thinking punk, cause I'm mentally challenged and he's colored we can't count. You don't know how many shells are in this gun. In all of this excitement I believe I may have forgot myself. You've got to ask yourself one question, do you feel lucky? Well, do ya punk? Like my old grandpappy used to say, 'Fagive but never faget'. I ain't gonna faget what you done to my colored sister," as he squeezes the trigger and blasts Jose backward watching him slide down the wall and fall over Malik. Jimmy walks over to Malik who is barely breathing and screams in his ear, "Show me the money!" C.A.N. smiles at Jimmy and tries not to laugh.

Sony and Susie who are in separate rooms on the other side of the house hear the gunshots and run toward the sound. Sony and Susie find their two partners lying on the floor.

Sony yells, "What the hell?" He calls Jose and Malik. They don't answer. Sony goes over to check their pulses and finds they are not breathing. Sony, with a terrible look on his face says to Susie, "They are fucking dead! Who could have done this shit?"

"Whoever fired those shots."

"You are right. That's explains why the alarm was turned off. There are keypads all over this house. They must have known the code."

Looking around the room to see if any other items were taken Susie comments, "They must live here because it doesn't seem like they were here for a heist."

"That black chick, the maid must have done it. I didn't see her with a gun. She must have had help."

"I told those assholes to stick to business! See what thinking with your dick will get you?"

"We need to split this scene".

As they head toward the front door, Sonny and Susie hear a car start up in the garage and then the sound of a garage door opening. They run to the front door and see the car pulling out of the driveway and onto the street with Jimmy sitting in the rear seat looking at the house as the car drives away. Sonny, seeing Jimmy in the backseat says, "Damn, they are a bunch of kids. Let's go after them. As Sony and Susie run out of the house towards the van Susie suddenly realizes and asks, "What about our friends in there?"

"Ain't nothing we can do for them now. I want to get my hands on those fucking kids!"

The Crew, drinking their milk as the car cruises down the street, are not driving fast because they are unaware that the van is following them. The van begins to get close to the Crew's car and bumps and rams the back of their car. Jimmy drops his milk and he falls forward hitting his head on the front seat. C.A.N and Sandy spill their milk too.

Looking in the rearview mirror and seeing the van C.A.N says, "Buckle up." Sandy reaches in the back of the car to help Jimmy fasten his seat belt and turns around and fastens her belt.

C.A.N. tells Jimmy, "Get the 12 gauge."

Jimmy looks down on the floor sees several guns that they took from the gun closet and says: "Which one is that?"

C.A.N., "That long black one." Sandy looks at C.A.N and smiles, unbuckles her seat belt and grabs the shotgun from the back.

Sonny confidently proclaims, "We've got them now."

C.A.N tells Sandy, "Give the boy the gun, he knows what to do."

"Ya, I been watching TV," Jimmy boasted.

Susie, riding in the passenger seat of the van, looking at the boy says, "That kid looks retarded."

"He does look kind of stupid ... but remember they killed our friends back there."

Jimmy, looking back at the van says, "A man has got to know his limitations," and shoots through the window of the van. Sonny is hit in the shoulder and Jimmy laughs as Sonny loses control of the van. The van drives up on a lawn and crashes into a bay window of a big nice house. The van crashes into the dining room where a rich white family is hosting a fancy diner party for wealthy friends. The Catholic Priest is about to bless the table full of food.

The Priest says, "Our Lord please accept our thanks" when the loud noise of the van crashes through the window. The crash startles the guests and they run for cover as the van drives through the house smashing into the table scattering dishes and destroying furniture.

Jimmy is laughing hysterically watching the van crash through the house.

Sandy says to C.A.N., "He is crazier than you."

"I'm not crazy, I'm mentally challenged."

C.A.N. smiles as they head towards downtown. As they get closer to town they pass an unmarked police car parked on the side of the road. The officer on the driver's side picks up his radio and ask headquarters, "What is the description of the suspected vehicle?"

The dispatcher responds, Answer, "1969 Black Dodge Charger."

Stan, the officer behind the wheel says to his partner, "Joel, that's it."

"Give them some room. Don't follow them too close. They might lead us to their crash pad where we can take them by surprise."

Stan, rejecting the suggestion, "The hell with that. They have taken out members of organized crime, whole gangs, police and anybody who gets in their way. Hell, they led Sheen on a wild goose chase and made him crash his own car. I've got orders to kill this man."

"Under whose authority? I thought we were told to bring him in alive. That boy is supposed to be retarded. If we kill that boy we'll lose our badges."

"The way I heard it, back at that house. it was the boy who did all of the shooting. Hell, the boy is just as dangerous is that crazy ass nigger."

"Come on, Stan. He must be a bad influence on that boy, teaching him aggressive conduct and the partaking of violent behavior."

"What the fuck are you now some police psychologist now?"

"I've been studying for the Sergeants' exam."

Stan, laughing, "The way you smoke and drink, you'll never live to see the day. Besides you would have to change your name. They are only promoting minorities. Right now we've been promoted to nigger chasers."

As the Crew get close to the city, Stan steps on the gas and they get closer to the Crew.

"Remember our orders, alive."

Stan, sarcastically says, "Sure alive."

Sandy looks in the backseat at Jimmy who is staring out the window at the unmarked car and says, "Here comes somebody."

"They have been back there for awhile, this car is marked." The crew speeds around a corner and turns into an alley.

C.A.N. orders, "Get out of the car."

Sandy says as they are getting out of the car, "We can't beat them on foot. We need another car."

The officers speed around the corner looking for the Crew. "Where did they go?"

C.A.N. flags down a yellow cab and snatches the driver out, throwing him to the ground and flips him a $100 bill. The Crew jump in the front seat with C.A.N. behind the wheel and begin to pull off when a group of Chinese tourists, two men and a female with cameras around their neck jump into the back seat. The man, with a heavy accent asks, "Coulda youa takea usa toa?" He doesn't finish his statement before C.A.N. notices the officers behind them and steps on the gas taking off suddenly slamming the new uninvited passengers to the back seat.

One of the guests in the back seat questions, "Whatsa going ona?"

"It's all good. We are making a movie, **'Shaft'** and pointing her finger at the tourist saying, "Bang bang."

The tourists, thinking that they are really making a movie jump up and down in their seat laughing and saying, "Hesa black man, hesa Shaft. Shafta, banga bang.

The cab is flying around corners, going through red lights as they are being chased by the officers. The tourists are still laughing jumping up and down saying, "Shafta, banga bang."

Sandy and Jimmy sitting in the front, are enjoying the activity of the tourist in the back seat … looking back and saying, "Movie, that's right, Shaft, bang bang."

In the meantime, Stan is frustrated. "I can't get a shot off because of those people in the backseat. What is all that jumping up and down about? Everybody who comes in contact with this maniac becomes crazy like him."

Sandy talking to the tourists, "Ya, those cops back there are in the movie too, Shaft, bang bang".

The tourists looking back at officers and pointing their finger at the officers like a gun, laughing jumping and down and saying, "Shafta, banga bang".

Stan asks Joel, "What in the hell are they doing?"

"They are pointing their finger at us."

Stan, with his gun out of the window says, "No shit, Sherlock, I can see that you idiot. A cab full of retards, niggers, a retarded cracker and a bunch of fucking Chinks.

Yelling at Stan, Joel asks, "What the hell are you doing? You can't shoot. You might hit the wrong people."

"You're right, but I can shoot the tires. You can always shoot the tires." He shoots and hits the rear right tire on the passenger's side.

Sandy screams. "Shit!" as the cab begins to sway side to side. Jimmy and the tourists in the back seat sway with the motion of the car. C.A.N. holds onto the steering wheel tight and maintains control of the cab.

C.A.N. says to the tourists "Y'all really want to be in this movie?"

They reply, "Yesa. Shafta, banga bang."

C.A.N tells one of the male tourists, "Take this right here," handing him a gun. "Now, point it at the actors back there playing the role of cops and shoot. It's ok they are just blanks – rubber pellets."

The tourist points the gun at the officers and says, "Shafta, banga bang." He squeezes the trigger. The gun goes off with a loud bang and the bullet goes through the rear windshield of the cab and shatters through the front windshield of the officer's car.

"What the fuck … these people are crazy!"

The Crew in the cab laughs as the officers lose control of their car and it flips over and slides down the street behind the cab upside down. The tourists in the back of the cab laugh even harder saying, "Shafta, banga bang."

The tourist shoot again as the police car continues to slide upside down behind the cab. The pellet blows one of one of the tires off the police car. The tourists are now in hysterics as they say, "Shafta, banga bang." Sandy is looking back watching the madness as C.A.N. continues to drive the cab on three wheels.

"Why in the hell are they still shooting at us?"

Stan says, "They are just fucking with us now. I didn't sign up for this kind of shit!"

Joel said, "Who are and where did he hook up with those Chinese people? They can't be tourists."

"Who in the hell knows. They are just as crazy as those niggers."

The tourist shoots again, blowing off another tire as the rest of the tourist crew in the back seat fall all over each other laughing. C.A.N. looking into the back seat at the tourist says, "Y 'all must be going for an Oscar." The tourist shoots again, blowing the muffler off the car. The tourists are dying laughing as they say, "Shafta, banga bang."

The tire that was shot on the cab now falls completely off and sparks fly as the bare metal from scraps the pavement. The cab sways even harder back and forth knocking the crew around in the back seat as they die laughing. The police car sliding upside down comes to a halt. The doors open slowly, the officers exit, crawling from the vehicle very slowly and stand up swaying & staggering because they are a bit shakened up and dazed. The officers look around for the cab but it is nowhere in sight. Stan walks over to the curb and sits down and says, "This is a bunch of shit."

Joel, standing in the middle of the street says, "Shouldn't we call this in?"

"Go ahead, call it in. Explain this to headquarters Mr. Police psychologist."

Down the street, the cab pulls over and lets the tourists out. They continue to laugh as they exit the cab saying, "Shafta, banga bang. Nicea moviea. Wea movia stars now."

Sandy shouts, "Y 'all the real shit. But don't quit your day jobs."

Jimmy smiles and says, "Bye-Bye."

The tourists wave goodbye as the cab pulls off saying, "Shafta, banga bang."

"We are going to need another car."

"Can we get a new one this time, like an E-Class or a LS?"

C.A.N.'s response, "We are out of milk."

Jimmy wanted to know, "Can we get candy?"

The crew sees a small used car lot with a small brick building for an office. Ribbons and flags decorate the lot. C.A.N. tells Sandy to drive and they switch places as she drives the cab into the car lot. C.A.N. lies down in the front seat of the cab with his head in Sandy's lap. Jimmy lies down in the back seat. Sandy pulls down the sun-visor to look in the mirror to straighten her hair, put on lipstick and sprays on perfume.

The car salesman, a young black man dressed in a nice suit comes out of the building and sees the cab all beat up and missing a wheel. The salesman, John begins to approach the cab and Sandy sees him approaching and gets out with her purse swinging on her shoulder before he can see C.A.N. and Jimmy hiding in the car.

Sandy walks toward the salesman, John. John, staring at her breast asks, "How can I help you pretty young lady on this fine day?"

"Ya, I want to check out an E-class, I mean I want to trade my car, I mean cab on an E-class, like that black one over there".

"Sure, baby doll, let's take it for a test drive shall we?"

"We don't have to do that. My mind is made up. How many dead presidents does it take to drive it home today?"

"Sounds good to me. Let's go into my office and discuss the numbers. I'm pretty sure we can come up with a figure that we both can live with." He puts his hands on her shoulder and escorts her inside the building smiling the whole time as he admires her sexy body. "Have a seat right here pretty lady," as he goes and sits behind his desk. Sandy notices that on the wall behind his desk is a board with all the keys to the cars on the lot. Sandy sits down spreads her legs so that he can get a better look. With a wide grin on his face John asks, "How were you expecting to pay for your E-class?"

"I do believe that my credit is good enough to negotiate for some dead presidents."

"I happen to have a loan application right here," as he reaches into his desk drawer to get the application. Sandy jumps up and slams his hand in the draw and he screams out loud, so loud that C.A.N. hears it and raises up his head to see what's going on. Sandy hits salesman John over the head with her purse causing him to fall back against the wall. The board with the keys on it falls on the back of the salesman's heels so hard that he yells again.

C.A.N. hears the second yell, gets out of the car and says to himself, "What the hell is she doing in there?" The keys on the board fall all over the floor and Sandy recognizes the Mercedes Benz keys, snatches them up off the floor and runs toward the door. Seeing her heading toward the door, John jumps on her back and they both fall through the door, down the steps and tumble onto the ground. They tussle rolling around on the pavement for a few seconds. John gets the best of Sandy by getting on top of her and slapping her in the face. Sandy fights back the best she can.

John says, "Think you were going to come and steal a car off my lot? You crazy bitch," and slaps her again.

"I'm tired of you skeezin ass bitches trying to take advantage of an honest brother. Y'all wouldn't go to a white man's place of business and try this shit," and slaps her again. He raises his hand to slap her again ... crunch, he screams as Jimmy bites a chunk out of his hand. John screams, "What the fuck was that?" looks up and sees Jimmy standing there with a part of his hand in his mouth and C.A.N. standing behind Jimmy.

John tries to get up, but C.A.N picks him up by his neck, twirls him around in the air and body slams him hard to the ground rendering him half conscious. C.A.N picks Sandy up off of the ground and helps her straighten up her clothes. C.A.N. begins to carry her away when she jumps out of his arms, runs back to the salesman who is still lying on the ground and kicks him between the legs and says, "I ain't no skeeza."

Sandy pulls up her skirt, squats over John's face (C.A.N. and Jimmy are watching, trying to figure out what the hell she is doing) and does a number two on the salesman head. As the crew walks away, C.A.N says, "What kind of T.V. shows you been watching?"

"Wild Kingdom! she answers.

C.A.N. opens the trunk of the Mercedes and sees a bag. Opening the bag he discovers it is full of weapons and puts it in the front seat of the Mercedes as they all climb in and drive away. They drive for a few minutes and then pull over to a curbside vendor selling hot food and snacks. They get out of the car and go over to the vendor. C.A.N. reaches into a cooler and pulls out several small plastic jugs of milk. Sandy gets Oreo cookies and Jimmy gets a bag of Twizzlers.

While the Crew is in line to pay for their food, a young Puerto Rican male attempts to snatch Sandy's purse and run. She hangs onto her purse as the perpetrator tries to run. Sandy screams as she is being dragged away. C.A.N. and Jimmy turn around and see her being dragged. C.A.N. runs and catches her, grabs her by the arm, untangles her from the purse and then runs with the purse in his hand as the perpetrator still thinks that he is dragging Sandy. The perpetrator turns around and sees C.A.N. hanging on to the purse and not Sandy. He tries to let the purse go but C.A.N. snatches him by the arm, picks him up and twirls him over his head finishing with a body slam onto the hood of a passing car.

The car comes to a sudden stop. A young white kid gets out and looks at the perpetrator stuck on the hood of his car and then looks at C.A.N. who gives him a cold blank stare. The kid, shaken by C.A.N.'s look gets back into his car and speeds off with the perpetrator still stuck on the hood. The car travels about 100 feet down the street when the perpetrator falls off.

The Crew gets back into the Mercedes and drives down the street eating their snacks and drinking milk. Sandy, looking around on the dashboard and console asks, "Does this ride got a CD player? I don't see one. It must be in the trunk." She sees the cassette player on the console and says, "It has a cassette player and I have a cassette tape." She reaches into her purse and pulls out a cassette of rap artist, Mystical, and puts it into the player. As soon as she puts the cassette into the player they hear a gun go off. The bullet strikes the mirror on the driver's side, knocking it off the door.

C.A.N. yells, "What the hell?"

"They shooting at us again," Jimmy answered.

Sandy, looking to see where the shots are coming from says, "Damn, it's that man."

"What man?" as he looks back and sees it's the salesman, John from the car lot driving a Mercedes sedan.

John yells out the window. "Nobody steals one of my cars, kicks me in the ass, bites my hand off and shits on my head. I'll show you crazy ass niggers who y'all dealing with!" and with his hand extended out the window he shoots again. This time the bullet hits the rear windshield of the Crew's car shattering the glass. Jimmy gets hit in the face from the shattered glass while looking back at the salesman.

C.A.N. opens the sunroof and says to Sandy, "Take the wheel." They switch places while the car is moving. C.A.N tells Jimmy, "Get down."

"Can we play Shaft again?" Jimmy gleefully asks.

"Get down, boy."

Jimmy lies down in the back seat. C.A.N. reaches into the bag of weapons and pulls out a pump action twelve gage shotgun. C.A.N. stands up through the opened sunroof. The shoot-out is on. Both the Crew and the salesman are flying down the highway each in a Mercedes.

C.A.N. tells Sandy, "Push it." She steps on the pedal and the car picks up speed while rap artist, Mystical is singing 'Come And See About Me.' C.A.N shoots at the salesman. The blast hits the grill of the car knocking the Mercedes emblem off the hood causing the car to swerve side to side. C.A.N. pumps the shotgun again and shoots. This time the blast knocks the passenger side mirror off the door.

The salesman shoots back, but misses. The salesman and C.A.N. are blasting at each other until they both run out of ammunition. The salesman reloads his 38. caliber handgun while driving.

C.A.N. instructs Sandy, "Hand me another one."

She opens the bag and sees several guns and asks, "Which one?"

"It doesn't matter, darling. Any one of them will do. Give me the Mac. Hurry up, Sugar!" She hands him another shotgun. C.A.N. and the salesman blast at other again until they run out of ammunition again as they drive through a tunnel.

Seeing that he ran out again, Sandy hands him a six shooter and a bottle of milk as the salesman reloads. The two exchange gunfire as the salesman follows the Crew around a corner. The cars lean into the curve and forces C.A.N. into the inside rim of the sunroof hurting his ribs.

The salesman shoots and the bullet hits the front quarter panel of the Crew's car. John aims for the Crew's car and the second shot blows the milk out of C.A.N.'s hand. Angry, C.A.N. fires off two shots. The first grazes the hood of John's car. The second hits the top front grill and blows open the hood. Sparks, fire, smoke and steam come from the engine of the salesman's car. The open hood prevents John from seeing causing the car to swerve each back and forth between the lines on the road.

He struggles to keep his car under control as he sticks his head out of the window to see around the open hood. The front right of the salesman's car bumps the rear left side of the Crew's car causing it to bump into and scrape the wall in the tunnel. Sparks fly causing C.A.N. to hit his right side of his rib on the inside of the sunroof.

John smiles because he realizes he has the Crew pinned and sliding against the tunnel wall. He turns his steering wheel to the right to keep the Crew pinned against the wall. Sparks continue to fly from the engine of John's car while sparks continue to fly from the Crew's car as it scrapes the tunnel wall.

Sandy holding on tightly to the steering wheel, nervous and scared asks, "What you want me to do?"

"Stop the car, darling."

"What?"

"Just stop the car, sugar plum." Sandy hits the brakes causing the car to slide for a few seconds and then comes to a complete stop. The salesman's car keeps going forward and because his steering wheel is turned to the right, it slams into the wall at an angle. C.A.N. sits back down into the seat and tells Sandy to back up away from the wreck. She slowly drives around salesman John's car and rubbernecks to check things out.

Groggy, the salesman staggers out of his car and raises his hand to shoot but C.A.N. quickly shoots first knocking the gun out of his hand. The Crew's car drives past the salesman as he stands in the tunnel watching them drive away. Seconds later he notices their car comes to a complete stop. The salesman notices the bright break lights in the tunnel and sees the white reverse lights on the car as they backup down the tunnel. John, nervous and scared begins to run.

Sandy looking through the rear view mirror as she is backing up sees the salesman running and says, "Don't be scurred you gonna get served." John tries to run away before the car driving in reverse to catches up to him. As they get closer, he falls to the ground. C.A.N.

gets out of the car, goes and stands over the salesman lying on the ground who is looking up at him. C.A.N. reaches behind his back as to pull out a weapon.

John begins to beg for his life saying, "Man I just wanted my car back. I have to pay for that thing." C.A.N. looks at him and pulls something from behind his back. John ducks and covers his head with both arms thinking he is going to be shot. After a few seconds he looks up and sees the man standing there with a bottle of milk in his hand. C.A.N. hands the bottle of milk to the salesman and walks backwards to the Crew's car. Staring in disbelief, John watches the Crew drive away through the tunnel for few seconds and says to himself, "Those niggers are crazy and pours the milk out on the ground."

Seeing him pour the milk out, Jimmy reports, "He poured it out." The car's brake lights light up bright in the tunnel, then reverse lights come on. The Crew's car backs up towards John. He doesn't run this time. He just stands there watching the car back up. C.A.N. gets out of the car, walks over to him with one of his hands behind his back like he has a weapon or another bottle of milk. John thinks it is a bottle of milk. C.A.N. pulls out a loaded pistol and puts it at his head. John is surprised to see that it is a pistol and drops to his knees.

C.A.N. puts a gun to John's head and says, "Kids are starving all over the world and you are pouring out milk. Lick it up!"

Again, John hesitates. C.A.N. nudges him with the pistol, but John still doesn't lick up the milk. C.A.N. pulls back the hammer on the pistol with his finger on the trigger.

Sandy and Jimmy are watching the whole scene from the car. Sandy jumps out of the car, walks over to the salesman, takes off her underwear and pulls up her skirt and placed her ass over the salesman's head saying, "So you don't want to lick it up. How about some more?" John looks up and sees Sandy's ass and quickly laps up the milk. Jimmy, looking through the back of the car window laughs.

John laps up the milk for a while and hears a man's voice say, "Are you all right, Mr.?" The salesman looks up and sees a white police officer looking down at him.

House Crashers

The officer reaches toward his belt where his gun and equipment are situated. Still scared and nervous, the salesman ducks and covers his head thinking that the police officer is reaching for a gun. The police officer reaches for and pulls out his radio and calls dispatch. "This is officer Stansfield. Please send a tow truck to the D-street tunnel along with the specialized care psych unit. We have a fellow here who may need psychiatric care."

A tow truck, ambulance with paramedics and more police arrive on the scene. Representatives from the psych unit put John in a straightjacket and escort him to the ambulance.

Sheen says, "Hold on. Let me talk to him". Sheen asks John, "Tell me what happened."

John, looking crazy says, "This crazy ass woman came to my car lot and tried to steal one of my best Mercedes. When I tried to stop her a boy bit my hand and some crazy ass nigger picked me up in the air and swung me around like a merrygo-round."

Sheen, staring at the salesman in a very strange way says, "Go on."

"Then the woman who tried to steal the car shit on my head."
"Why were you licking the ground?"
"I had to lick up the milk I poured out."
"Why is that?"
"Cause, if I didn't lick up the milk she was gonna shit on my head again."
"Take him away."

Chapter Twelve

THE CONNECTION

Police Chief, Stewart and Sheen are discussing the recent activity in the tunnel. "Sheen, I heard the call on the scanner in my office, it sounded like our milk man is at it again. What do you have for me detective?"

"We got a call about shots being fired in the neighborhood of Georgetown."

"That is a very nice neighborhood. There hasn't been a serious crime committed in that area in over thirty years. Did we identify the caller?"

"Yes, the call came in from neighbors who said that they heard shots coming from the house next door. According to the neighbors, the original owners of the house were out of the country. Of course, when we arrived we found two bodies and another wounded victim. The same MO ... that crazy ass milk man, retarded boy and a girl who hasn't been identified yet."

Chief Stewart asks, "What was that address again?"

Sheen, handing the chief the written note says, "Here it is, Chief. It was at this address. Things have changed."

"What do you mean?"

"When I was a boy, we couldn't even go into that neighborhood."

"You are right. I remember now. About 30 years ago, my second year on the force, we received a call from that same location. I do believe it was that same location about a robbery of some sort. When my partner and I arrived on the scene it was awful. Evidently, a milk truck was shot up real bad and the driver was killed. But, if I remember correctly no money was taken. The strangest thing was that the driver was black. That was very odd in those days because as you mentioned certain ethnic groups, including blacks were excluded from that neighborhood, even though they lived there prior to the whites."

"It is beginning to make sense now."

"Oh yeah?" the Chief questioned.

Sheen responds, "Yeah! I believe the suspect's father was a milkman. Back at the old lady's apartment we saw a picture on the wall of a milkman with a woman and a young boy. Those must have been his parents. The little boy in the picture … that must be him. That also explains why he is always asking for milk."

"Yeah, in your reports, I read where the surviving victims stated that the suspect always asked for milk. That must be his connection to that neighborhood. Somehow, some way, he must have known the owners of that house because it is too much to be a coincidence."

Sheen asked, "Did you say money was not taken from the scene thirty years ago?"

"That's right. We did not find any evidence of robbery and the money collected on the route was accounted for. It was still in the bag. It almost appeared to be a hit."

"Why would anyone put a hit on a milkman?" Sheen asked shaking his head.

"Things were crazy in those days. He must have been uncooperative with the people who taxed everybody, if you know what I mean."

"Yeah, but a milkman!"

"It's that or some white extremist group sending a message …I don't know."

"What kind of a message?" Sheen asked.

"For people like you and I to stay out of that neighborhood."

"That's an awful way to send a message."

"Remind me to tell you a story about why my parents left Mississippi."

The Connection

"Sheen, my parents were from the south too."

As they walked out of the office together the Chief says, "I need to share this new information with the police psychologist."

Communicating with representatives from the records and files department on the phone, Chief Stewart inquires, "How long do we keep records or files on old cases? Yes, this case was never solved. It was a shooting that left a milkman dead on the scene. It happened my second year on the force. Very funny. I ain't that old. Well, whatever you have it on, micro-film, computer disc or whatever, I need it right away."

Chief Stewart, in the office with the police psychologist says, "I believe we finally have a break-through in the case involving that mad man with the milk."

"Oh, yeah! What do you have, Chief?"

"Another case that happened a long time ago that might strangely be connected to our mad man."

"An old case? How so? What case?"

"About 30 years ago we received a call about a robbery in a real high dollar neighborhood and when we arrived on the scene, we found a milk truck all shot up, and the driver was killed. We found the driver slumped over the wheel."

"That must have been an awful scene, Chief. Tell me why someone would rob a milk truck? Did they confiscate the milk? I can only imagine there was not a sufficient amount of money to take."

"Awful? Yeah it was! There was milk and blood everywhere and strange as it may sound, no money or anything of monetary value was taken. Most of the milk was destroyed by gunfire."

"Let me see the file." Chief Stewart hands her the file.

"My, this reads like borderline insanity. But, I don't follow you, Chief on where the connection is for our mad man."

"Look at the lead detective's report, Doc. Look at the address where the episode occurred at that house. Now look at the old case file. Notice the address of the house where the 911 call was placed. It's next door to the house where the call came from and we think the connection is the mad man. The milkman was his father. And the apartment where the officers were killed, there were pictures of a family, a man, a woman and a little boy standing in front of a milk truck. It was the same milk truck that was shot up thirty-years ago and the man we found slumped over the wheel is the same man in the picture."

The psychologist looking into the Chief's eyes says, "Are you sure? That was a long time ago!"

"Of course, I'm sure. It was my second year on the force and the first time that I ever witnessed a scene like that. And we were surprised that the man was black because Blacks were not allowed in those neighborhoods. The detectives at that time suspected the shooting was racially motivated."

"Well, I guess the detectives did not have to spend much time on the motive."

"Yes, but they were wrong, because we found out later that it was a mob hit."

"A mob hit?"

"Doc, during those days, the mob controlled everything, even milk and other produce delivery routes. The word on the street was that the man had taken over the route from an old milkman who did pay the mob for the use of the route and it's my guess the new milkman refused to pay … so they sent a message. Our mad man is the milkman's son."

"Chief, it is my professional opinion that every time he places himself in a position to hurt the bad guys and help innocent victims, psychologically, he revenges his father's death and resurrects his father's life. And in a little boy's mind, a cartoonmind, he is ridding the world of evil. Chief, he must have witnessed his father's death or has visions about it in his head. He will continue to go after people who have wronged others. He will kill again and again until the T.V. is turned off in his head."

"I thought about it for a long time, and I still don't understand the T.V. scenes. Why does he carry out or try to relive these T.V. scenes?"

"The T.V. serves as a teacher or a counselor of some sort. He seeks consolation through the characters that are motivated by revenge, thus providing him with psychological stimulus to the brain which triggers hidden forces to rid the world of evil. In his eyes the world is the people who have suffered an atrocity like him. As I stated, it almost makes me want to believe that he may have witnessed the event. He may have seen his father being massacred and his repeated violent activities demonstrate revengeful manifestations."

"Do you have any ideas how we can stop him? We thought that with the boy and now the girl traveling with him that would slow him down, or at least make it easier for us to catch him."

"Might I suggest that you consider setting a trap for him?"

"A trap, what do you mean?"

"Chief, you could stage a crime or some type of criminal activity and let the bad guys get away. The criminal activity must be believable. It must be against humanity and/or innocent victims."

"Humanity, what exactly do you mean?"

"The activity must be negatively appealing to him in order to trigger a positive response, meaning it has to be appalling and shocking enough to make him want to help or be revengeful. It must trigger or appeal to his emotions to the point where he can relate to it, especially if it relates to his childhood. I suggest the act be against poor people, the under privileged children or against the elderly. Your undercover officers could pose as bad guys who carry out criminal activity and leave an easy trail for him to follow them to a place where he can be caught. Set it up where he can easily approach. Or wait until another crime activity occurs. Have your officers put a tail on the bad guys and just wait until he shows up in an effort of what he feels is the notion of ridding the world of evil … and when he comes for the bad guys … nail him. Another way to surely get his attention is to capture the boy and or the girl. Do it without harming them. It seems he has substituted the girl and boy for the family he lost and has incorporated them into his notion to rid the world of evil. And if he does consider these people his family, and in if indeed they are the only family he has, he will surely try to get his family back. If my theory and psychological diagnosis is correct, he will definitely come to their rescue. Chief, you need to raise the stakes in order to strengthen the bait, *so to speak.*"

"Chief, you also want to ensure that the people you use to set up this trap are the best you've got. They must be your most experienced. One false move or any indication of suspicious activity or characters he will unearth the situation and pull back. This man may even become agitated or view the whole situation as an insult to his intelligence, which has demonstrated to arouse his anger, resulting in more violence."

"Do you think this idea will work? It sounds risky."

"As you know, Chief, there is a risk in everything we do. But, it can be done successfully. It can work. Psychologically, we have to negate his notions and accentuate his will and desire to act. Chief, we can use that in our favor and also rely on his own determination and strength of character to be used against him. I know it can work Chief, if your people are good and follow your instructions. The main instruction would be to give this man a chance to follow his desire. That will place him in a vulnerable position and then eliminate his ability to act or react to the trap. Chief, the trap must be fail safe. It must be set up where the apprehension is swift. He must fall into the trap. As stated, Chief you're going to need your best on this one. Train them if you have to, but make sure they are ready and most importantly, you are going to need people that you can trust … especially considering the political ramifications. And knowing the mayor, he wants this man alive. You must make it work."

"That's what we used to call 'Netem'. When I was a rookie on the force, we use to work in teams. A couple of cops would bait the suspect out in the open and me and my partner would always drop a tight net over the suspect before he could have a chance to react. We would club him before he could reach for a weapon. Given the way this suspect manages to get out of the most difficult situations and predicaments that ordinarily would have been unescapable, we might have to consider a more drastic measure, hopefully without severe results. Yes, you are correct, the mayor wants him captured alive and brought to trial."

The Connection

"Well, Chief, you seem to be experienced in criminology and the suspect's modus operandi. Hopefully, you can accomplish your task and fulfill the mayor's request. Politically, it should be a feather in your cap."

"I really don't need another feather in my cap and I will not be politically correct if I can help it. Drastic situations, especially under extreme conditions, sometimes call for drastic measures. I will instruct my officers to protect their own lives if and only if it comes down to it. I will allow them the flexibility they need, but order them to shoot to kill only if they have no choice."

"Be careful, Chief. Everybody, including the political brass, is closely watching this whole thing because of the fan club and community support he has earned. My little nephew, my sister's son, has one of those t-shirts and every time I go to the market, I can't even get milk for my coffee. Whatever you do, do not under estimate this man. He may be crazy, but so far he hasn't demonstrated the actions of a human being of low intelligence."

C.A.N. and his crew have now left the scene from the tunnel and are driving down the street in their beat up, noisy, smoke-blowing Mercedes. C.A.N says, "We need a new piece of transportation. But … first let's find a place to live for a while."

"Hey, I know. My aunt, Gawanda, she has a place in northwest. She'll let us crib there for a little while."

Jimmy asks Sandy, "Does she have a T.V. set with color?"

"Yes, and she even got cable and a DVD player and that surround sound stuff."

C.A.N. chimes in with a question, "Does she have?"

Sandy interrupts him before he can finish his question and says, "I don't know. But, yes, she has a refrigerator and she should have milk."

"Turn down this street. Turn down this alley." The Crew rides down the alley behind a row of nice townhouses. "Pull in here. This is her spot."

They pull into the parking garage and turn of the car. As he exits, C.A.N. finds himself looking down the barrel of a loaded pistol. The pistol is pointed right in his face. He stops in his tracks. Jimmy also comes to a complete halt. The pistol is being held by a beautiful black woman, in her mid-forties who is tall, slender, athletically built with beautiful long hair. She is dressed in casual lounge athletic sportswear and white tennis shoes. C.A.N. is motionless, Jimmy says, "Mrs. Ma'am we are here to look at T.V."

Gawanda looks at C.A.N. and Jimmy and asks, "Who are you crazy ass niggers?"

"We are middle class Negroes," Jimmy retorts.

Sandy, who was slow getting out of the car after C.A.N. and Jimmy says, "Aunt Gawanda, it's me, your niece, Sandy."

Gawanda with pistol still pointed at C.A.N looks over at Sandy and says, "Child, what on earth are you doing here?"

"Aunt Gawanda, these are my friends and we need a place to crib for a minute to get cleaned up. People are after us. We need to chill for a minute."

"You all are those crazy ass niggers all over the T.V. news. You all can't stay here. You shouldn't have come here to put me in the middle of your mess."

"Come on Aunt Gawanda. We've got nowhere else to go. It will only be for a minute."

Gawanda, looking at the Crew says, "If it wasn't for the fact that you are my brother's child, I would leave you right in the street and who is this crazy little white boy?"

"I ain't crazy. I'm mentally challenge!"

Gawanda looking at C.A.N. says to herself, "Damn, this nigger is fine. I might keep him for myself." She lowers her pistol, turns around and walks toward the house and says, "The things you do for family."

Sandy looks at C.A.N. and Jimmy and says, "I told y'all she was cool."

C.A.N., looking back as Sandy, says, "Cool, right."

The Crew, led by Sandy, follows Gawanda up the sidewalk and into the back door of the house. Reaching the second floor living room and family room areas Jimmy is immediately drawn to a big flat screen T.V. He is amazed at the size, shape and width (thinness) of

The Connection

the T.V. and measures the width (thinness) of the T.V. with his thumb and index finger. He holds up the width portrayed by his fingers up to the light, moves the measurement of his fingers back and forth close to his face as if to say, '**What a thin T.V.**'

Gawanda notices and announces, "That boy is obsessed with that T.V. Hasn't he seen a T.V. before?"

"Not like that," Sandy answers.

Gawanda looking at C.A.N. asks, "Where did y'all get him from? He must be from green acres or somewhere like that."

Gawanda asks Jimmy, "Hey boy, what is a middle class Negro anyway and what makes you think that you are a middle class Negro?"

Jimmy sharply responds with, "Cause we drink white Zinfandel, eat our chicken with a knife and fork and listen to Johnny Mathis records."

Jimmy receives a strange look from Gawanda as he approaches the stereo continuing, "When my Pa wasn't around, we sneaked off and listen to colored music."

Everybody looks at him with a look of what the hell are you talking about. Jimmy pushes a few buttons on the stereo and Wilson Picket's record "1000 Dances" comes on and he starts to do the country jig. C.A.N. smiles and asks Gawanda, "Do you have any milk?"

Gawanda answers, "No, I don't have milk in the refrigerator, but I can make you some." Gawanda goes into the kitchen, opens the cabinet door, reaches up in the cabinet and pulls down a black & white box placing it on the countertop. She opens another cabinet and pulls out a glass blender, opens the refrigerator and pulls out a container of water. She pours the white powder from the black & white box into the blender along with the water from the container. She turns the blender on mixes and the formula turns a milky white. C.A.N. and Jimmy hears the blender mixing the formula, they both peep into the kitchen.

C.A.N. looking back at Sandy whispers, "What the hell is she doing in there? I only wanted milk."

"Oh, my aunt ... she is a health nut."

C.A.N. looks at Sandy strangely as if to say 'what the hell are you talking about?' Gawanda pours the formula into a big glass and takes it to C.A.N. Sandy turns her head and smiles because she knows what's about to happen. C.A.N. stares at the glass, sees that the formula looks like milk, turns the glass up to his mouth and drinks for a few seconds. Then his eyes get large. A crazy look comes over his face as he chokes and then spits it out. The formula sprays all over the place, all over Gawanda and the floor. His face turns pale and he acts like he has to spit up but belches real loud and pushes out a loud long fart which catches Jimmy's attention. C.A.N. trembles and shakes, and tries to walk forward but falls back down on the couch as he says, "That ain't no milk."

Gawanda proudly states, "That's better than milk. I mixed it myself."

"Mixed it! What the hell are you ... some kind of mad scientist?"

"No, of course not! My formula is healthier then dairy milk. It doesn't have cholesterol, steroids, and additives and all those other chemicals they feed them cows that causes cancer and all those other medical problems that we suffer from."

C.A.N., lying on the couch looking as white as a ghost says, "I don't know about chemicals or steroids but milk ain't never bothered me. It ain't never made me sick. Milk is good for you. That stuff you made will kill you faster than any milk I've ever known about. That shit is rough. Sandy is smiling and trying hard not to laugh. Anybody chooses that stuff over milk will surely die from that taste.

Gawanda, speaking softly, "Sorry that you didn't like it. I don't mind the taste."

"That shit is rough, but I appreciate you going through all the trouble to make it, mix it or whatever you did. I didn't mean to mess up your house."

Gawanda offers, "That's alright. Let me get something to clean you up and this mess you made."

"Sandy, please get some towels and help me clean up this mess."

Gawanda begins to wipe C.A.N. with a towel while Sandy cleans the floor. She glazes into his eyes as she wipes his face and mouth and says to herself, "This brother is fine. I sure would like to…" and begins to fantasize about making passionate love to him. The fantasy in her mind takes place in her bedroom. She is wearing sexy lingerie that expose her breast. She and C.A.N. are on a large bed laced in silk with candles and incense burning around the perimeter. Barry White is playing in the background. She is on top of him making passionate love while he is sucking her breast. In her mind this goes on for a few minutes until she sees a hand on her arm, she stares at the hand for a few seconds and realizes its Sandy pulling on her.

"Aunt Gawanda, Aunt Gawanda, he's clean enough. You are going to rub the black off the man. You are going to rub the brother to death."

She looks at Sandy and pauses for a second, returning to reality says, "Oh, I'm so sorry, I just wanted to make sure he was clean."

"He's ok, Gawanda. He's good."

C.A.N. joins Jimmy who is watching T.V. and can't help but glance over at Gawanda who herself is glancing at him. Sandy catches the glancing and shows an expression of anger and jealousy.

Chapter Thirteen

THE PLAN

Chief Stewart is in her office on the phone talking to Police Captain Steve Isiroe. "Captain, we need to talk. I'll be right over."

In her long, blue unmarked sedan she is being driven through the streets she is expected to serve and protect while trying to wrap her mind around the kind of plan to do just that. Arriving at the local precinct, she gets out of the car with the hope that Captain Isiroe agrees and can help with the execution of that plan. This is what they will discuss.

Chief Stewart, upon arrival to the Captain's office starts the conversation, "Captain, as I stated on the phone, I have met with the mayor and our psychologist who is supposed to be an expert in criminology. We are going to need your best and most trustworthy detectives and officers on this one."

"Whatever we have to do to get the job done. You will have **whatever** you need, Chief. What's the plan?"

Captain, remember, we need him alive. The plan is to capture him alive."

"I do have some experienced officers that can accommodate any situation. When it comes down to police work our detectives here are very good, but to capture him alive, Chief I can't guarantee that. What if this maniac pulls out a gun and starts shooting? You know as well as I do, our people are trained to shoot back, especially when their lives are in danger or the public is at risk."

"Captain, I do understand the importance of the protection for your officers. I had your job once. But the mayor is pushing for a trial so the public can see that the system still works. That is why I want and need your best to handle it and not some trigger-happy officers that can't handle themselves under pressure situations like this one may turn out to be."

The Captain, being sarcastic, smiling says, "I suppose the mayor has a master plan?"

"Very funny. Let's talk about the plan. I was hoping you, we could set a trap for him. Set it up where he comes to you and throw or drop a net over him before he could react. Your officers will have to act fast, but whatever you do don't allow him time to think or react. Net him as soon as he shows up on the scene. Make sure the net is tight and heavy ... you know, the type that will pin his arms and legs, restricting the probability and his ability to fight back."

"Chief, you are talking about the use of the net gun instead of a stun gun. We use a gun now that shoots the net over the perp that not only knocks him down, but also grabs the perp so he can't get loose or fight back."

"Oh yeah, I believe that's it."

"Yes, Chief, the officers work as a team. One officer will shoot the net over the perp while the other officers pin the perp down to apprehend him. It's an action that happens simultaneously and a method that has proven to work effectively with excellent results."

"Good, it sounds like we can apprehend this mad man and bring him in to stand trial. This will make the Mayor and City Council happy. It will demonstrate to the public that we are still in charge and can do our jobs effectively, as well as give the prosecutor an opportunity to really earn his paycheck. And it will surely keep me out of the Mayor's office, for a while anyway."

"Chief, I've got to ask you."

"What's that?"

"Do you miss the action? They say that you were **the man** back in the day."

The Plan

"I miss the streets and the people we helped. We had a better relationship with the people. They respected us. People in those days were more supportive and respectful toward the men and women in blue until those damn hippies showed up. The people really appreciated us keeping their neighborhoods safe. Little old ladies would give us fruit baskets and bake us pastries to show their appreciation. Families would invite us into their homes for coffee or tea. Kids would emulate us … always wanting to see our guns. We didn't have special interest groups or greedy lawyers screaming police brutality. Things were a lot simpler in those days and better for cops. Now these young punks kill each other over what they think is their turf or for crack or other bullshit. We didn't have guns that shoot nets. We wrestled them to the ground and kick the shit out of them."

"I bet you didn't have to deal with maniacs like this one."

"The closest we ever came to this maniac was when I was working in New York City. I was assigned to the search detail for the Son of Sam case. We never did catch him in the act. He was found through a parking violation AND he was not seen as a hero like this maniac. The people of New York feared the Son of Sam. These people think this fool is a hero and walking around wearing those damn tee shirts idealizing him."

"Chief, my lead detective, Sheen, said and it's also right here in his report that this fool is traveling with a girl and a little retarded boy. If that's true I can't guarantee that they won't get hurt, I can only minimize the risk."

"That's why I'm asking for your best and most experienced be assigned to this case. They may have to take them all down if they are with him at that time, and believe me, you don't want to hurt that retarded boy, regardless of anything."

"I can see the prosecutor trying to defend us on that one."

"No prosecutor can fix it or protect your men from the press and those damn special interest groups if that boy is killed. Social services will have a field day and the Mayor will have both our jobs."

"You know, Chief, this whole precinct, me included has respect for you, but you are asking a lot on this one."

"I really appreciate your respect and I know you and your officers work hard out there, but it is not my request, it is the Mayor's. This can be a political nightmare if we don't play our cards right. I'm not asking you to compromise the safety of your officers or the integrity of this department, but we need them alive."

"We will get them."

"That will be great."

Chapter Fourteen
IMPLEMENTATION

Still hanging out at Gawanda's house, C.A.N. and Jimmy are sitting on the couch watching T.V. The movie is The Matrix. They are into the scene where the girl dressed in black flies through the air over the building across to the roof top and Jimmy says to C.A.N., "Can you fly like that?"

"That's what they call special effects done by movie makers in Hollywood. Nobody can fly like that! Superman couldn't even fly like that."

Sandy chimes in, "Flying off a building is easy, (smiling) it's that sudden stop that kills ya."

Gawanda, walking over from the kitchen asks, "What are y'all talking about?"

"These fools talking about flying," laughs Sandy.

Gawanda, looking at the T.V. says, "I've seen this movie a bunch of times" and sits on the couch beside C.A.N. She grabs the remote control and begins flipping through the channels stopping on a local news station.

"Gawanda, we don't want to see no news stuff," Sandy shouts.

"Y'all need to pay attention to what's going on in the world. You just might learn something."

The news is a story of some hoodlums wearing masks robbing a local charity event for black orphans. C.A.N. is watching this story with disgust. His face is sad and his eyes show a cold evil look. During the commercial Gawanda says, "That is a shame! You can't even have a program for children without somebody messing it up. Who on earth would do a thing like that … rob poor children?"

C.A.N. gets up from the couch and walks toward the door. Gawanda yells, "Where are you going?"

"To get some real milk."

"Milk?"

"You are going after those bamas that robbed that children's program aren't you? I know you, C.A.N., screams Sandy.

Gawanda chimes in, "Why are you doing that? Let the police handle it. They should be able to catch them thugs."

C.A.N does not respond. He just looks straight ahead with a serious and evil expression on his face.

"Wait for me. I'm going too. You ain't leaving me. I want to be there when you clock them bamas," Sandy insists.

"Girl you are crazy. You better leave those people alone and let the police do their jobs. If they are crazy and roguish enough to steal from poor children there's no telling what they will do. Who could do such a thing? They couldn't have a conscience!"

"I know who it was," Jimmy asserts.

Gawanda, looking at Jimmy with a puzzled expression says, "You do? Who are they?"

"They are like the Grinch," responds Jimmy. "Grinch?"

"Ya, you know like the Grinch that stole Christmas?"

C.A.N. loosens his expression, smiles at Jimmy and says, "You are right."

Jimmy smiles back and says, "And I want to go too."

"You stay here with Gawanda. Both of you stay here."

Sandy, getting a little angry yells, "I want to go! You are going to need somebody to watch your back anyway."

"No, it's not safe for y'all anymore."

"Girl you'd better listen to that man. He knows what he is talking about."

"I ain't scared of them bamas. I can handle my shit."

Implementation

C.A.N. smiles and says, "You can definitely do that. You've proven that already."

Gawanda looks at both of them with a puzzled look on her face and says: "What are y'all talking about?"

Jimmy speaks up and says, "When we went to buy a new car the man didn't want us to have it, so she pulled."

Sandy abruptly interrupts, "You need to learn how to stay out of grown folks conversations."

Gawanda, shaking her head, "I really don't think I want to hear the rest of that story."

Sandy gets her coat to leave – makes an attempt to go with C.A.N who turns around to see her. "I thought you understood. It's not safe for you out there. I need to work alone on this one."

Sandy gets an attitude, starts to pout, takes her coat off and slams it into the closet, walks over and flops down on the couch and folds her arms and turns her head toward the wall.

Jimmy, feeling a bit sorry for her offers up his support by asking, "Do you want to watch SpiderMan?"

"No I don't want to watch no damn Spider-Man."

Gawanda walks C.A.N. down the steps and to the back door. As they get to the back door she stops and looks into his eyes, hugs him, kisses him and says, "Please come back."

"I'll be back. You watch over them. You watch over my family. And don't feed them none of that formula. That stuff will kill them."

Holding his hand she asks, "How do you know where to find these people? They are probably long gone by now."

He smiles and walk towards the door. "I need transportation. I need to borrow your car."

"I'll get the keys." She turns to go inside for the keys while Sandy sneaks out through the front door down the sidewalk.

Sandy walks in front of the house talking to herself, "He ain't going to leave me here."

Gawanda gets the keys from the upstairs bedroom, brings them downstairs and out the back door handing them to C.A.N. He gets into a black BMW 750li, pulls out of the garage and drives down the alley.

Meanwhile, Sandy enters the garage from the opposite side and gets into the Mercedes they drove up in and follows him from a distance.

Back upstairs, Gawanda notices that Sandy is not there and asks Jimmy, "Where is Sandy? Where did she go? She was supposed to stay here." Jimmy just shrugs his shoulders.

Gawanda, with a worried look on her face says: "I pray that she isn't trying to follow him. I have a real bad feeling that wherever he is going, it won't be safe for her."

Sandy is following C.A.N. from a distance in the Mercedes that's running kind of rough. C.A.N. drives for a little while and then pulls over to the side of the curb on a busy street where several young black men are standing. Sandy pulls over about a block behind. The window of C.A.N.'s car rolls down and he talks to some brothers for a few seconds, and hands one of the brothers a roll of dollar bills who passes back a brown bag and a sheet of paper. Sandy is watching the whole scene from where she is parked on the street. C.A.N. nods to them as he pulls away from the curb.

Implementation

Sandy continues to follow him from a distance. She drives slowly by the same curb and stares at the brothers as she drives by. The brothers hear the Mercedes and stares back at her as she drives by. The brothers are too well casually dressed to be hoodlums, but don't really look like cops either. Sandy notices that the man who gave C.A.N. the brown bag and the piece of paper walked around the corner talking on a cell phone. She continues to follow C.A.N. from a distance for a few minutes until they approach a warehouse district. C.A.N. slowly drives into the warehouse, makes a few turns and then parks the car. He reaches into the brown bag and pulls out a gun and places it inside his rear waistband. Opening the car door, looking around he walks towards one of the warehouse buildings. One has a few cars parked in front of it and a sign on the side of the wall that reads **Wonderland Toys** with little toys and colorful balloons around the sign. C.A.N. walks up to the door of the building, tries to slowly turn and twist the doorknob, but the door is locked. Sandy is watching the whole scene from a short distance as he reaches into his pocket and pulls out a set of pick locks. He picks the lock for a few seconds, and finally gets the door unlocked. Slowly the door opens and he enters the warehouse. On the rooftop of the adjacent building is a white man wearing a dark colored uniform similar to that of a S.W.A.T. uniform. The uniformed man is speaking on a cell phone and communicates, "He just entered the building."

The voice on the other end asks, "Is anyone with him?"

"Not that I can see."

Good, come on down and join the party."

"Roger that. I will be right there" and he disappears.

The inside of the warehouse is almost dark with shadows of retired machinery piercing the lighted areas. On the loading dock are five men loading a truck and discussing the toys that they took from the robbery.

The leader says, "Make sure that the Williams family gets the 200 boxes because they already paid for them. The rest of the loot, you guys divide amongst yourselves."

"Sure thing, Sam."

The loaders turn around and see C.A.N standing staring at them with a bottle of milk in his hand. He never takes his eyes off the loaders as he raises the bottle of milk to his mouth and drinks the last of it and lowers the empty bottle of milk down to his side. The loaders stare at each other for a few seconds.

Sam yells out loud, "Now!" A man standing back in the dark area holding a strange looking gun shoots out a big net over C.A.N. knocking him to the floor.

Sam shouts again, "We've got him. Secure him, men!" As the loaders rush over to secure him, he quickly reaches into his pocket.

Sam sees his action and yells, "Watch it men, he has a gun." The loaders pull back as he pulls out a knife and cutting instrument and begins to cut his way out of the net. He quickly slices and dices his way out as he gets up from the floor.

The loaders watch in amazement as he cuts, slices and dices himself out of the net. In amazement.

Sam speaks with the only thing that comes to mind. "Jesus," as he watches C.A.N. in action.

Free from the net he attempts to run for cover and as he runs, one of the loaders yells, "I got a shot."

"His leg, hit him in the leg." The loader shoots him in the leg. He stumbles, almost falls to the floor, but stays on his feet and runs limping out of sight to a safe area. Things are quiet for a few seconds. Sam and the loaders take cover as they huddle together in an area of the warehouse that is slightly dark.

Sam talking to the loaders, "Should we tell him we are cops? He might give himself up."

"Give up? After what the cops did to his mother? We have a snowball's chance in hell that he'll give up."

Sam, again speaks out, "Men, we've really got to cover our asses on this one. We've got to play it by the book. It was expressed by the brass to bring him in alive. We've got to give him a chance, I mean an opportunity to surrender."

"We got a wounded man on our hands. He could be dangerous. The word on this maniac is that he is crazy. You saw the way he

Implementation

cut through that net. I don't think he'll give up," asserts one of the other men.

"I've got orders to try and bring this man in alive, if at all possible."

"That may be difficult, Sam."

"I know that, but I hand-picked you guys for this assignment because of your experience in this type of situation. I convinced the Captain that this team could bring this man in alive. If we play our cards right that wound to his leg can work in our favor. He's going to need medical attention. We can use that as a bargaining chip. Let's keep him pinned down for now," Sam urges strongly.

He then reaches into his pocket and pulls out a headset with a microphone, plugs it into his ear and contacts the Captain. Speaking in a low tone to her, Sam informs her of the activity thus far. "He slipped through the net (pause). Don't ask. We put a bullet in his leg to slow him down."

Back in the precinct the Captain explains to the doctor who helped hatch this plan, "He managed to slip through the net, but took a bullet in the leg, they now have him pinned down."

"That doesn't sound good, Captain."

"I think I should send backup."

"That might complicate the situation even more. The officers need to keep the suspect calm and keep themselves calm as well. The calmness may prevent him from reacting in haste," advises the doctor.

The Captain instructs Sam while looking at the psychologist, "Sam keep the situation under control. Try to keep him calm. Try to reason with him for his surrender. Give him a way out. Give him an opportunity to surrender with dignity. He will take any kind of insult as a threat, which might provoke him to react violently. Do what you have to Sam, but try to coax him into surrendering, but, as a last resort, take him down."

"Okay, Captain. We are prepared to coax him into surrendering. I just hope that this "head" game will work. I'll try to appeal to his senses.

Confidently, the doctor speaks up, "I am sure it will work."

"Alright men, we have our orders. It's official. We have to push for his surrender." The pretend loaders now confirmed as officers look around at each other with one reluctantly saying, "Roger that."

Sam yells over to C.A.N. "Hey fella, we would like to talk to you about this situation. We know you are hurt, but if you work with us we can end this right now and no one else has to get hurt. We need you to surrender. If you come out right now, I give you my word no further harm will come to you." No response.

The officers look around at each other. One of the officers says to Sam, "You think he is still over there? He may be unconscious."

"Are you over there, my friend? Can you hear me?"

C.A.N responds with, "Top of the morning to you fella."

Sam and the other officers look at each other with the expression on their faces as to suggest '**What the hell**'?

"Hey fella, you talking to me?" C.A.N questions.

"Yes, my friend."

"Do you have any milk?"

Sam and the officers are stunned as they look around at each. Some of the officers smile and giggle. The officer closest to Sam says to Sam, "Did he ask for milk?"

Another officer pipes up with, "That nigger's crazy. Why in the hell would he want milk at a time like this?"

Sam says, "A better question is where in the hell are we going to get milk?"

"Nowhere, Sam. Let's just take this fool now while we've got him out numbered."

"Sorry fella, that's an order we cannot fill. But you are welcome to come with us. I believe we can get you all the milk you want," Sam encourages.

C.A.N. yells back, "Sorry fella, I ain't going nowhere until I get some milk."

One of the officers notices that there is an office inside the warehouse with a big square window and through that window notices there is an old big white refrigerator. The officer taps Sam on the shoulder and points to the refrigerator. A couple of the officers

Implementation

crawl on the floor to the refrigerator and opens the door to discover a milk carton. One officer gets the carton and shakes it to see if it contains milk and it does. The officer gives a thumbs up to Sam to signal that the carton does have milk.

Sam turns around and begins to speak to C.A.N., "Hey fella, I think we can fill your order. Now come and get your milk. I promise nothing is going to happen to you. We can wrap this thing up."

"Hey fella, this ain't **Red Rover**, and I won't be coming right over. You bring it over here."

Sam, with milk carton in his hand slowly stands up and looks over toward the area where C.A.N.'s voice is coming from. He pauses for a moment. The other officers are questioning his sanity. "Sam, what the hell are you doing? That fool is going to kill you."

"According to the police profile on this man he hasn't hurt or attacked anyone who didn't pose a threat to him. He hasn't hurt any innocent people yet." Sam moves slowly towards C.A.N.

"Sam, don't be a fool. Don't be another one of this man's casualties."

"Be cool, men. It's going to be alright."

"Cover him."

The officers position themselves. They brace themselves, re-grip their weapons to back up and cover Sam. Sam talking to C.A.N. as he slowly approaches with the milk carton announces, "Hey fella, don't shoot. I am coming to bring your milk that you asked for."

"Hey fella it's all good. I just want the milk and it better not be made from no box." The officers look at each other as if to say, '*what the hell is he talking about*? Not knowing C.A.N.'s exact position they stay focused on Sam and the area where the voice is coming from. An officer watching Sam slowly move across the floor says, "He is just as crazy as that crazy ass nigger."

"I am here. I have your milk. Where do you want it?"

"Bring it over here." C.A.N. stands up slowly from his position, but doesn't approach Sam. He stays in the background and steps forward just enough to show his face. He and Sam look into each other's eyes, staring at one another for a few seconds as if they have seen one another before.

Sam says, "You, it's you." The officers covering Sam are a bit nervous because they can't see exactly what is going on. They can only see the back of Sam. Suddenly, a man appears through the skylight glass window on the ceiling with a scope rifle. It's a sharp shooter sniper on the roof. The rifle is aimed at the back of Sam. The sniper is trying to aim and shoot at C.A.N. but Sam is in the line of fire between the sniper and C.A.N.

The sniper on the roof, appearing through the glass skylight says to himself, 'Come on, Nigger. Show me your face.' Sam and the other officers aren't aware of the sniper on the roof. The officers are still focused on Sam while Sam is focused on C.A.N.

Sandy who has been hiding in the dark watching the whole scene the entire time slowly appears from the dark from behind C.A.N. She sees Sam but doesn't see the other officers, but sees a shadow on the floor that is from the rooftop. Sandy looks up and sees a sight glimpse of the sniper on the roof appearing through the skylight.

She stares at the image for a second and realize that it's a man with a rifle taking aim at the location where Sam and C.A.N. are. The sniper still talking to himself is begging, "Come on cop, move out of the way." When Sam leans forward and bends over just a little bit to hand C.A.N. the carton of milk the sniper re-adjusts his position and re-focuses his rifle and says, "That's it cop move just a little more."

Sandy watching the whole scene realizes what is about to happen, runs out from the dark to warn C.A.N. shouting, "It's a set up. It's a set up."

Sam, surprised and startled looks at her with an expression of **'what the hell'**. It is a confusing situation. C.A.N., Sam and the officers

Implementation

are still unaware of the sniper on the roof. They are concerned about Sam's safety and Sandy is trying to save C.A.N. from the sniper's bullet. Concerned for Sam, the officers fire on Sandy knocking her backwards when she is hit by the officer's bullets. For a brief second the sniper gets a clear shot of C.A.N. but as he squeezes the trigger Sam stands up straight and the sniper's bullet hits him in the back of his shoulder. The sniper is mad because he missed his target and says, "Shit."

C.A.N. looks up quickly and in that brief second recognizes the sniper as the same man that shot him in the hallway of his apartment building.

The force from the sniper's bullet knocks Sam forward into C.A.N. Sam drops the carton of milk but before it hits the floor C.A.N. catches it and places it in his mouth holding it between his teeth. He grabs Sandy with one hand and Sam with the other and drags them both to safety. He, Sam and Sandy are now lying on the floor. Sam is shaken but still alive and Sandy is bleeding badly.

Sam looks up at C.A.N. and says: "I believe I took one in the back."

C.A.N. looks at Sam for a few seconds and says: "Thanks for the milk." The officers are puzzled. They know they shot the girl but don't know if Sam is dead or alive.

One of the officers calls out, "Sam, are you alright? Are you hit?"

"Stand down, men. Stay where you are."

"You guys cover me. I'm going to check on Sam."

The officer begins to crawl on his elbows and knees towards the area. Sandy is lying on the floor dying, bleeding to death from the officer's bullets. C.A.N is down on his knees holding her in his arms and looking into her eyes, her face is full of blood. He pours the milk over her face and then wipes her face clean with a cloth from his pocket. Looking down at her with tears in his eyes he says, "I thought I told you to stay put." Now the tears are flowing down his face. "You were supposed to stay back there with the boy. You are so damned hard-headed."

"And miss all this action ... you know better than that. I told you, you ain't going nowhere without me." Lying on the floor next to them, Sam is watching the scene.

Sandy begins to choke from the blood in her mouth.

Trying to be strong and keep it together C.A.N. tells her, "I got to get you to a hospital."

He makes an attempt to lift her, as he begins to stand the officer that crawled on the floor over to where they are is now standing over him with a gun pointed right at his head says, "Don't move." C.A.N., still holding onto Sandy, stays in a crouched position.

"I've been waiting to meet you face to face. So you are the maniac? You've developed quite a following. There are people who want you alive. Obviously, there are some of us who want you dead." He looks around to see if anyone is watching, pauses for a second and cocks the hammer on his gun.

Sam, lying on the floor, in a weak voice says, "Stand down, officer. This man pulled me to safety."

The officer ignores Sam and begins to squeeze the trigger. With the loud sound of gunfire, the officer is still standing but now with a hole in his head. He falls backwards.

Sandy, still in C.A.N.'s arms is holding a gun with smoke coming from the barrel. She drops the gun and says in weakened voice, "I told ya it was a set up. Did I get that bama?"

C.A.N. just stares into her eyes with great sadness. Sandy, looking over his shoulder and up to the ceiling says, "They forgot to pay the light bill. It's getting dark in here." As C.A.N lowers her body to the floor she looks up at him asking, "Did I ever tell you, you are one fine ass nigger? Make love to me one more time, Daddy." With tears in her eyes and a smile on her face she speaks, "Hey, I see Grandma. Grandma, wait." She smiles at him for the last time, closes her eyes and says, "Grandma" and passes away.

Sam, lying on the floor with tears in his eyes says to C.A.N: "Get out of here, and take your family."

"Thanks again for the milk," responds C.A.N.

Chapter Fifteen

Home Coming

Jimmy is in the second floor window looking down at C.A.N carrying Sandy's person. He screams with excitement, "They are back!"

Gawanda rushes to the window and sees C.A.N carrying Sandy's limp body. He stops and stairs up at Gawanda. They stare at each other for a few seconds and tears begin to flow down Gawanda's face. Jimmy stands there with a blank look on his face.

The psychologist and the Chief of Police, Sally Stewart have reconvened in the Captain's office. They all have blank expressions on their faces because they are not sure what to make of what just happened back at the warehouse.

"Do we know what happened?" the Chief asks.

"From what I understand from the officer's report, everything was going as planned. It seemed the officers were on point until the suspect cut his way out of the net. According to them, they were able to keep him calm and it appeared that he was ready to surrender, especially when they were able to fulfill his request for the milk," responded the Captain.

"They had milk?" asked the Chief.

"No, there happened to be a refrigerator in the warehouse office that had a container of milk."

"We were lucky on that one. What about this sniper I read about in the report?"

"Apparently when Sam, the lead officer, was brave enough to carry the milk over to the suspect a girl, the one that you warned us about Chief, came charging out of nowhere toward the officer. The backup officers, trained to protect the point man and not knowing the girl's intent or unaware of the total situation, thought that she was going to attack Sam. One of the backup officers fired on the girl."

"Was she armed? Was she carrying a weapon? Did anyone see the girl with a weapon? This is very important! Come on, Captain. Talk to me!"

"It was dark in that warehouse, Chief and according to the officers I spoke with stated it all happened so fast."

"Did she have a weapon or not?"

"I don't know, Sally. The officers didn't say and it wasn't in the report." The Chief looks at the psychologist and then looks at the floor and shakes her head.

"Chief, you have to understand, it was dark, she came running out of nowhere and the officers did what they were trained to do. Based on the situation, it was a legitimate and justifiable response," the Captain offered.

"What about this sniper?"

"Again, looking over the situation, it seems now that the girl may have spotted the sniper on the roof and came running out to warn the suspect. From the ballistics report, the trajectory of the bullet that entered Sam's shoulder may have been intended for the suspect. The girl must have seen or at least sensed what was going to happen and tried to stop it, trying to save her friend. Sam may have been in the line of fire."

The psychologist finally chimes in with, "Guys, it seems that someone else or entity wants to stop this man."

"You mean kill this man because someone wants him dead?"

"It appears to be the case," says the doctor.

"Chief, this man has had scrapes and altercations with several groups associated with criminal activities," adds the Captain.

"Activities, you mean blood baths?"

"You're right, Chief, and the sniper may be connected to any of those groups?"

"What happened to the girl?" the Chief continues her inquiry.

The Captain answered, "After the smoke cleared, the officers could not find the girl or the suspect. He must have taken the girl with him. It is unconfirmed, but we believe the suspect took a bullet in the leg. We've got officers posted at every hospital just in case he goes for medical treatment."

"I thought for sure this would be over by now or at least I had hoped so," added the doctor.

"We did plan to catch him. We planned on having him in custody by now. The officers said the way he sliced and diced through the net he must have had some type of military training."

"My professional assessment tells me it could have just been rage or fear. We are not dealing with an ordinary man here folks. Chief, his personality profile will change now," warns the doctor.

"What do you mean?" Sally asks.

"Instead of ridding the world of evil, he will now adapt to ridding evil from himself."

"What the hell are you talking about?" the Captain asked with a puzzled look.

"Don't ask," the Chief responds with sarcasm.

"Well, instead of being reactive, he will now become proactive. He will be in an attack mode. Do we know if he knew about the sniper?" asks the doctor.

"At this time we don't know that fact. Why?"

"If he knows about the sniper or knows who the sniper is, he may go after the sniper. And if not, he may channel his rage at the police," continues the doctor.

After a measured silence the Captain says, "Chief, we have to take off the kid gloves. We must stop him now. I need the order for neutralization."

"Neutralization, what does that mean?" questioned the doctor.

"Don't ask," said both the Chief and Captain harmoniously.

The Chief, looking at the Captain, says, "I will get back to you after my visit to City Hall."

The Chief and the psychologist leave the room and walk out of the building. The Captain uses his cell to place a call. Speaking on the cell in a very angry tone, "You almost got my best officer killed today. All bets are off. If you sent a sniper, what the hell do you need me for? That crazy ass nigger could have killed all my men. Your man fucked up. He missed and hit my officer and I had to modify the reports to cover it up. In case you didn't hear me the first time, it's over. I'll handle it from here. What, because of your mistake. Fuck you. I have to kill this nigger to prevent him from retaliating against my men. I don't want your fucking money. That's your problem. You fuck with me I'll turn your whole organization upside down."

Chapter Sixteen

THE GRAVE

The graveyard is nice, clean and is well-manicured with pretty green grass. The graves are well kept. The graveyard is surrounded by a black iron fence and double gate. C.A.N., Jimmy and Gawanda are standing over a casket with flowers on it. C.A.N. and Jimmy, dressed in suits, are looking straight ahead while C.A.N. is holding a large black Gucci bag. Gawanda, dressed in a very fine dark outfit is crying over the casket. Amongst them is an elderly black minister wearing a black suit, white shirt and black tie, a gravedigger and two pallbearers dressed in jeans. The minster is presiding and delivering the eulogy. Gawanda is weeping softy while the minister says, 'Young, so young, so many of our young brothers and sisters leave this world way to soon becoming statistics of evil even before they can experience what life really has to offer."

C.A.N looks at the minister as if to say you did not know this girl. As the minister continues with the eulogy, two four door dark sedans pull into the graveyard through the iron gates. The crew, not facing the gate, does not see the cars enter into the graveyard, except the grave digger. The cars stop about four rows (100 yards) away from where the crew is positioned. The doors of the cars open, a total of seven men emerge from the cars. Six white men and one black, dressed in fine suits, shirts and ties (mob looking) start walking slowly toward the crew. The gravedigger has been watching the cars the whole time enter into the graveyard and seeing the men approach, sensing something is wrong because there is no other funeral or grave burial scheduled. The gravedigger lowers his shovel to the ground and slowly moseys away. The minister, puzzled at the gravedigger's action, looks up and sees the men slowly approaching speeds up his eulogy and says, "Ashes to ashes dust to dust, Amen." closes his bible and says, "I make it my business to mind my own business, but in this case, for the Lord, I am going to make an exception. My good people looks like y'all got company," and walks off and says under his breath, "Lord, please don't let them or me become another statistic." Watching the minister's actions, the remaining staff follow suit.

C.A.N., looking down at the casket says to Gawanda, "Go, leave now and take the boy with you." Gawanda begins to turn around to see what is coming but C.A.N. says, "Don't look back. I don't want them to know that we know they are here. Take the boy and walk away and don't look back ... Gawanda grabs Jimmy by the hand to walk away but he tugs away from her because he doesn't want to leave C.A.N.

"Go with her, Jimmy. Go now, before it's too late. It's me that they're after." Jimmy breaks loose from Gawanda and clamps onto C.A.N.'s leg.

Trying to push Jimmy off his leg he says, "Boy, be a nice boy and go with Gawanda." But Jimmy hangs on even tighter. C.A.N looks at Gawanda and says, "Leave him. Go now."

Gawanda, crying, hugs C.A.N. real tight and hard, kisses him and whispers in his ear: "I don't want to lose you too. Please come back to me." Gawanda walks away in the same direction as the minister. As Gawanda walks away, she reaches into her purse pulls out a large makeup kit and accidently drops a lipstick container on the ground. She opens the kit to look in the mirror to see what's happening behind her. She positions and angles the mirror in order to see the men approaching C.A.N. and Jimmy at the gravesite.

She prays, "Lord, please watch over that fine ass nigger and send him back to me in one piece and the boy too."

C.A.N. tells Jimmy, "Let's pray." As they kneel down to pray Jimmy starts, "Our fatha who ain't in Heaven."

The men approach and one says to the other, "What the hell are they doing?"

The Grave

"Looks like they're praying."

"Praying? Good, they are going to need it."

While Jimmy is praying, C.A.N. opens the Gucci bag, and inside are weapons, automatic machine guns with clips of ammunition and handguns with back up clips. As he quickly loads the weapons he asks Jimmy, "Have you ever played cowboys and Indians?"

Jimmy responds, "Yes, can I be an Indian?"

"Okay, we are the Indians and those cowboys are sneaking up behind us. And not like on T.V, we are good Indians and we are going to win because we have real guns not bow and arrows like on T.V. We've got to shoot back until all of the cowboys are dead. Got it my little man?"

"Got it Chief Indian."

"No, my man you are the Chief".

Jimmy smiles and says, "I get to be the Chief? I ain't never been picked to be the Chief before."

"You're the Chief, now."

"Hot dog! I'm the Chief!" and runs off and disappears for about a second.

"Where in the hell did he go?" C.A.N. quietly says "Hey Chief, where are you?"

Jimmy suddenly appears out of nowhere standing next to C.A.N. with the lipstick Gawanda dropped from her purse in his hand. Jimmy applies two small stripes of lipstick under each eye.

"What are you doing?"

"Putting on my war paint. I'm Chief. I gotta prepare for battle."

"Chief, now that you got your mug together let's play and I know you know how to shoot."

"My Pa and me … we once shot a bear, but he kept onagoing."

"Well there is some two legged cowboy bears right behind us. When you shoot this time make sure they don't keep going."

"Don't worry, my Pa was marxeyman."

"What the hell is that?"

"You know, a marxeyman, a man that can look through a magnifying glass on the gun with a patch over his eye and his hat turn backwards and shoot anything that scadadles."

"Okay, Chief marxeyman."

"I am a good shot too. I can pluck the barnickels off a bullfrogs back at 100 paces and have his legs for supper".

"Damn, I hope you are good as you say you are."

The men continue to walk slowly through the graveyard, moving around the headstones – creeping up behind the Crew. The men can't really see what the Crew is doing. They don't know that the Crew is arming themselves and preparing for battle.

One of the men questions, "What are they doing?"

"Saying their last goodbyes," Another man replies sarcastically with a smirk on his face.

"Goodbyes, that just about sums it up."

The men begin to pull out their weapons, load them and prepare to attack the Crew. As they get closer they see that C.A.N. is with a little person.

"Who is that with him? Oh shit, it looks like a boy. "Maybe we should wait until he is alone."

"We have our orders. Let's do this thing and get it over with so we can collect on the contract."

The Crew still have their backs to the men creeping up behind them. C.A.N., handing Jimmy an automatic handgun instructs, "Take this one too, and put it in your pocket. When you can't shoot this big gun anymore, start shooting this little gun. Whatever you do don't stop shooting and remember as the Chief marksman, you must not let those cowboys win."

The seven men are now spread out in a line walking slowly toward the Crew with weapons in hand.

C.A.N., sensing the men are close has a quick flashback of his father being shot up in the milk truck and a serious, mean and evil expression comes over his face The Crew is now standing over the casket with their backs turned to the men creeping up behind them. C.A.N looks down at the casket, looks up to the sky and then looks straight forward across the landscape of the tombstones and says, "Chief are you ready?"

"Ready."

"On my command."

The men are now about 50 feet away. One of them raises his weapon and points it at C.A.N.

C.A.N. says under his breath, "Shoot me in the back, I don't think so" and shouts, "Now Chief." They spin around fast enough to make a tornado blush with guns ablazing. The bullets hit the man in the middle. The bullets spray his body, knocking him back about six feet.

Another, standing beside him is also knocked backwards yells, "Shit."

The remaining posse takes cover, ducking behind tombstones as they return fire. The Crew is still standing blasting away hitting tombstones, tearing through tombstones, ricocheting bullets bouncing every which way. It's obvious their guns are hi-tech, state of the art weapons. The bad guys are still hiding behind the tombstones and can only raise their guns over the stones to blindly shoot back the best they can. This goes on for about five minutes. Then the bad guys stop shooting back. C.A.N. raises his hand to signal to Jimmy to stop shooting.

"Gentlemen this is not working. We got to strategize. We need a better look to see what is going on. One of the guys cautiously raises his head to peep over a tombstone to see where C.A.N. and Jimmy are located and to see if they are wounded. He can see C.A.N. is still standing tall.

C.A.N. sees the head and drops his hand to signal to Jimmy to shoot. Jimmy hits his target shooting him right between the eyes causing the man to tumble backward a few feet. Jimmy says, "Marxeyman. One more down, five to go."

"They got us pinned down. We got to try and flank'em. Orlando work your way down to the left, try to get an angle on the boy. We got to take out the boy. You can handle him by yourself."

"No problem, I'll get the little bastard."

"We will eliminate the main target."

Orlando begins to crawl on his hands and knees down to the left staying behind the tombstones.

C.A.N. and Jimmy see what is going on. Jimmy whispers to C.A.N., "Hesa tryin to crawl away."

"No, Chief, they are trying to flank us. Chief, we can't let them flank us."

"I'll stop him from flaging us," and with weapon in his hand he starts to move. "Remember don't take candy from strangers." Jimmy squats down low and starts moving in the direction that Orlando is going, walking and ducking behind tombstones as he goes along talking to himself, "You ain't gonna flag me."

C.A.N remains in the same position and keeps his eyes focused on the position of the other guys. They decide to stay in their positions for a few minutes until one of them asks, "Are we going to just sit here and let him pick us off one at a time?"

"We need that flank, let Orlando get in position and then we take them out."

"It's too quiet. He's planning something. I'm not going to sit here while he figures out a way to pluck us off."

"Go ahead hot shot, do us all a favor and go over there and get him."

The Grave

"Cover me," The aggressor jumps up with machine gun blazing and charges toward C.A.N shooting at will.

C.A.N. stoops behind a tombstone and waits for his opponent.

The hitman stops in front of the tombstone where he thinks C.A.N. is hiding, peeps over the stone to shoot, but C.A.N. is not there. He is surprised to see no one there. He looks up and C.A.N. snatches the gun out of his hand.

C.A.N. looks at him squarely in the face and asks, "Did you bring some milk?"

Looking puzzled, "Milk? No, but if you are thirsty you can suck my."

Before he can finish the sentence, C.A.N hits him in the mouth with the butt of the gun knocking out his front teeth. Staggering, he walks back toward his posse with a very bloody shirt. Hearing his approach, one warns, "Someone is coming."

"Is it the target or our guy?"

The leader calls out to his friend, but gets no answer because his buddy can't answer. He cannot answer because he has something in his mouth. Looking over the tombstone to see who is coming one of the gang, recognizing their own shouts, "It's our guy."

"Why won't he answer? They must have cut out his tongue."

The leader looks up again and says, "Jesus Christ, it's worse than that." Their comrade finally reaches the rest of the posse and drops to his knees. They can see that his dick has been stuffed in his mouth and he falls over dead.

The leader with a disgusting look on his face says, "That nigger is crazy. I'm going to kill him. What in the hell is keeping Orlando?"

Looking down at the dead man on the ground, "I'm with you, boss, let's take this fool now. You and me, boss. We can take him. We don't need Orlando's flank."

"Are you fucking crazy? We need the flank position as a distraction. He can't take on all three of us. We'll wait for Orlando's signal."

Orlando is now in position where it appears that he has the angle on C.A.N. He crouches behind a tombstone and lays the barrel of his gun on the tombstone. Closing one eye to look down the barrel he takes aim at the position of C.A.N.

Jimmy has been following Orlando the whole time and sees what is going on and says to himself, "He's trying to be a marxeyman."

Orlando doesn't see Jimmy peeping over a tombstone. He raises up a little more to get a better look at C.A.N.'s position and takes aim to shoot but before he squeezes the trigger, Jimmy shoots, hitting Orlando's gun, knocking it from his hand.

"That's our signal."

C.A.N. hears the shot, but keeps his focus on the other two guys.

The leader and companion begin shooting at C.A.N. C.A.N. shoots back. Orlando picks up his gun and tries to shoot at Jimmy. The gun doesn't work so he pulls out another handgun and shoots at Jimmy.

"Ok cowboy you ain't gonna flag us," shooting back at Orlando.

Now there are two gun battles going on. C.A.N is mixing it up with the two bad guys and Jimmy is mixing it up with Orlando. All furiously exchange gunfire, shooting back and forth. C.A.N is blazing at both bad guys with a machine gun and they are shooting back.

Orlando and Jimmy continue to blast at each other. Jimmy is having fun at this game before they both run out of bullets. Having the second gun that C.A.N. gave him, Jimmy pulls it out and gets ready to use it. Orlando realizing that he is out of bullets and is pinned down says, "Hey boy, I know a nice kid like you would like to have a good ole piece of candy."

"Do you have milk to go with it?"

"Milk, where in the hell am I going to get some milk? No milk, but I do have a nice piece of candy."

"What kind of candy?"

"Butterfingers. See, look." and reaches into his pocket and pulls out a large Butterfingers bar and barely waves it above the tombstone.

Jimmy, peeping his head over the tombstone, "You don't have no candy."

"Yes I do," and waves the candy bar a little higher.

"I don't see no candy."

Orlando raises the candy a little higher until Jimmy can see Orland's whole hand. Jimmy sees Orlando's hand holding the candy bar waving it back and forth. Jimmy shoots bang and blows Orlando's hand off. Orlando falls to the ground screaming and squeezing his wrist where the hand is missing. He then uses his other hand to reach into his pocket to pull out a handkerchief and ties it around his wrist and tightens it using his teeth. In deep pain and in shock, Orlando walks staggering back towards the other guys. Jimmy, still pointing his gun at Orlando moves parallel with him ducking behind tombstones, watching and following his every move.

The two other guys look up and see their friend staggering towards them with a hand missing. "What in the hell? Not again!"

Their friend with the missing hand, obviously in a lot of pain, nervous, crazy and hysterical yells to the leader, "Give me a gun! Goddamn it! Give me a gun! I'm going to kill them both. Try to be nice to a kid and look what happens."

His partners in crime stare at their friend with the missing hand for a few seconds and one of them speaks up and says, "Damn, a kid did that? Jesus!"

Orlando, with his hand missing says crying, "Just give me a fucking gun!

The leader throws him a gun. He catches it with his one hand, turns around and shoots toward the area where the Crew is located. The Crew takes cover behind tombstones.

C.A.N. asks Jimmy, "What happened back there? I heard the shots."

"That cowboy, he tried to give me candy without milk. I knowed it was a trick, so I shot the candy."

"Chief, I think you shot more than candy."

"That's cause I'm a marxeyman ... oh and a Chief, too."

The shooting stopped while the hitmen reloaded their weapons. The leader helps 'one-hand' load his weapon, saying, "We have to finish them off on this go round.

This is the last of the ammo."

'One-hand,' in a demanding voice, "Leave the boy to me."

C.A.N. tells Jimmy as he is reloading their weapons, "Chief, I need your help one more time."

"Do you want me to stop the flag?"

"No, but those cowboys are really going to come hard this time, especially after what you did." He hands Jimmy a loaded weapon and says, "Are you ready?"

"This ain't basketball but I do love this game," says Jimmy. They stand up to get in a position to shoot.

The leader of the hitmen says to his partners, "Let's do it."

'One-hand' stands up and shoots first, but misses. C.A.N. already standing, hits one hand with a couple rounds and he falls over and lands face down over a tombstone. The Crew continues to shoot wildly at the bad guys with guns blazing and bullets flying everywhere. The bad guys are pinned down again. The leader tries to shoot back the best he can, but the Crew keeps blasting.

The other comrade who happened to be a black man, sees that they are pinned down and says to the leader, "Fuck this shit. Those niggers are crazy. I ain't going to die in no graveyard," and he begins to crawl away.

"Hey, you can't leave me here. What about the contract? What about the money?"

"Keep the change, boss."

"Hey, come back here, you fucking coward."

"Call me what you want to, but you can call me gone."

He tries to crawl away, but the leader shoots him in the back and says, "Fucking coward. I didn't need you anyway." The leader is now alone, thinks about his situation and yells over to the Crew, "Hey, can we talk about this?" You guys win. Let's call it quits and we can all just go home."

Jimmy says to C.A.N., "He probably don't have no milk and it is another trick."

"You're probably right, C.A.N. responds to Jimmy.

The lone rider and former leader of a now defunct posse yells out again, "Hey, what do you say over there?"

C.A.N. responds with an invitation, "Come over here. I want to talk to you and leave your weapon."

The Grave

"If you don't mind, I think I'll pass and just go home."

Again, C.A.N. extends his invitation, "I think you should listen to me and come over here. I just want to talk to you. I don't think you want me to send over my little friend. He ain't as nice as me."

"You, keep that little retarded kid away from me."

"I ain't retarded. I'm mentally challenged," and fires off a shot toward the leader. The bullet blasts passed the leader's head and strikes a tombstone behind him.

C.A.N. yells back at the leader, "I think you see what I mean."

"You made your point." He takes a handkerchief from his pocket and waves it in the air over the tombstone where he is hiding.

C.A.N. sees the handkerchief and says, "That's right, come over here and walk real slow and put them hands up where I can see them."

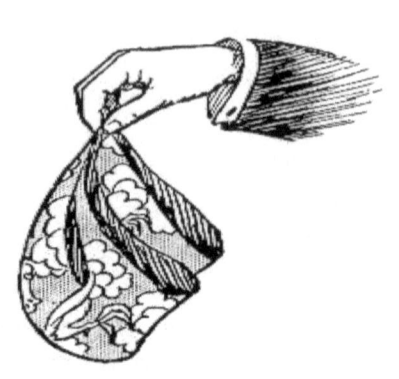

"Ya, put them hands up reala high and walk reala slow so I can count the lace holes in your shoes," chirps Jimmy.

Still waving the handkerchief, he rises very slow over the tombstone and begins to walk slowly toward the Crew with a shotgun behind his back and tucked in his pants.

"Raises both hands."

"I think my arm is broken, I can't raise it any higher."

C.A.N. says to Jimmy in a low voice, "If you even think he might move that other arm, if he even flinches, blast him."

The leader, looking kind of tattered is now getting close to the Crew.

C.A.N. says to the leader, "That's close enough."

The leader slumps down and leans on a tall tombstone and says, "I sure could use a tall glass of milk." The Crew looks at each other with blank faces and when the leader sees them take their eyes off of him for that split second he quickly reaches behind him and pulls out the gun and points at C.A.N. to shoot him.

Jimmy sees out of the corner of his eye what the leaders is about to do and quickly shoots him between the legs. The leader screams and falls to the ground holding his crotch. Looking at Jimmy wearing suspenders and warpaint on his face says, "You crazy little bastard!"

"I ain't crazy! I'm mentally challenged."

C.A.N. looking down at the leader says, "I told you, but you wouldn't listen. I just want to ask you one question. Who sent y'all after us?"

Lying on the ground obviously in deep pain, making faces he says, "Fuck you, you crazy ass nigger."

C.A.N. places his foot on the leader's crotch and applies pressure making him squeal out loud, "Man, I don't know. I just took the contract."

C.A.N. with his foot still on the leader's crotch looks at Jimmy and says, "Chief, what do you want to do with this Indian?"

"Leav'em for the buzzards."

The Crew begins to walk away while listening to the yellings of the wounded leader, "Hey, you just can't leave me here. I'm going to die."

C.A.N says as they walk away, "Fool, that's what graveyards are for … the dead."

The Crew walk to their car and as soon as C.A.N. opens the door to get in, a bullet rips through his shoulder. He grabs his shoulder, the same shoulder that was wounded in the apartment building. He drops to his knees between the car and the opened door. The bullet came from the same sniper that was at the apartment and the warehouse. The sniper takes his rifle apart, breaks it down and puts it into its case making a call on his cell phone. "It's done. It's all over."

"What about the boy?" The party questions, "Don't forget about the boy. You make sure it's done."

"It's done."

"Make sure. Check the body."

C.A.N. is on the ground bleeding, but still breathing. He looks up at Jimmy telling him, "Go boy, get out of here. Go ahead. Crawl away from this place and keep your head down."

The Grave

"You and me can get the rest of those cowboys. I'll help ya," and tries to move him but can't.

C.A.N. smiles at Jimmy and says, "You've been a good Chief. I'm proud of you. But the game is over now. We will only win if you make it out of this place. This place is a graveyard, but it doesn't have to be for you. So, go son, go now."

Jimmy, with tears in his eyes says, "You ain't never called me son before."

Jimmy hugs him tight and C.A.N. smiles through the pain as he hugs him back saying, "You have to go now, Jimmy. You have to go." Jimmy refuses to let go and C.A.N. says, "Come on now, son you must go before it's too late. If I don't see you no more in this world, I'll catch you on the next one and we'll have some milk together."

"Milk … you promise?"

"Yes, son. Remember to always drink your milk. Now go" and Jimmy disappears. C.A.N. is lying between the car and the driver's side door with his back and head against the door and legs on the ground. He is in deep pain as blood slowly pours out of his shoulder. But, there is a smile on his face because he is having flashbacks of the good times of his childhood, playing with his mother and riding in his father's milk truck. The flashbacks also include wild and crazy times with Sandy making love in the kitchen. And Jimmy riding in the back of the car saying bang bang, and the other people he avenged and the powdered milk at Gawanda's house. He is dreaming.

A shadow of a man appears over his body and disrupts his pleasantries. He opens his eyes and recognizes it's the sniper. The sniper stands over C.A.N. and pushes his boot on the fresh wound to increase the pain which causes more blood to ooze. This pain erases the smile from C.A.N.'s face.

The sniper says to C.A.N., "So you're the crazy ass nigger that everyone is making such a fuss about. You're the nigger that won't die. Well, my friend, you are going to die now and you don't even have any milk. What a shame!"

C.A.N. looks up at the sniper with a blank look on his face. The sniper sees that C.A.N. is still alive, raises his gun to shoot him and a loud gang sounds off and the sniper drops to the ground. Jimmy is standing on the roof of the car with a smoking gun pointed where the sniper's head was and says, "No more cowboys."

After shooting the sniper, Jimmy slides down off of the roof of the car, gets a bottle of milk from the car and places the bottle of milk up to C.A.N.'s mouth and helps him drink it.

C.A.N. stares into Jimmy's eyes as he drinks the milk slowly and begins to slip away. Before he slips away Jimmy helps him struggle to his feet. Once on his feet, C.A.N. hears the voices of his mother, father and Sandy coming from the direction of Sandy's grave. He looks off in the distance and sees his mother in a white nurse's uniform. His father is dressed in a white milkman's uniform and Sandy is in a sexy outfit. They are all standing over Sandy's grave. Jimmy doesn't see what C.A.N sees but watches him stagger with the last bit of his energy toward the gravesite.

With big smiles on their faces, his parents encourage him to keep coming, "Come on, son. You can make it. We have been waiting for you. Come on, son."

Sandy, with a bright smile says, "Come on, brother. You know you can't live in that world anymore. You'll never have any peace there."

C.A.N. continues to stagger through the graves in their direction. He falls down a couple of times. Jimmy runs over and helps him to his feet again. Again he falls. Finally he makes it to the gravesite crawling on his hands and knees with blood pouring from his shoulder. His mother, father and Sandy escort him into the grave as their spirits rise slowly to the sky.

As they fade into the sky, Gawanda, back in her house has a fuzzy vision of Jimmy walking through the grave yard all alone and she drops to her knees crying in sorrow.

The End

Heroes and/or vigilantes come in all shapes and sizes ... literally. Some you love. Some you love to hate. Dr. Hugh M. Weathers, a professional businessman, writer, educator, media specialist, producer, etc. introduced you to C.A.N.

Never has there been a character like this one. C.A.N. is a unique, quiet, yet explosive man. We are pleased you joined him on this journey of intrigue where we hope you were kept mentally challenged and emotionally exhausted. This ride of his lifetime allowed you to enjoy the many experiences that helped to make him the complex character that kept you riveted to this page turner.

You have witnessed Dr. Weathers' ability to weave an engaging story that should have left you wanting and waiting for the sequel. His talent has allowed him to deliver a fascinating novel that has captivated all that has had the opportunity to pick it up.

C.A.N. ... PULP COLORED ... THE MILKMAN is a masterpiece written by Dr. Weathers that has helped to encourage those that think they can't and support those that know they can. His *"can do"* attitude is only matched by his diversity and belief in doing what one loves. Writing happens to be one of his many talents that he enjoys and does well as is demonstrated by this work.

C.A.N., by your own experience ... hero or vigilante ... you be the judge.